HIBERNIAN CHARM

BOOKS BY DEAN F. WILSON

THE CHILDREN OF TELM

The Call of Agon
The Road to Rebirth
The Chains of War

THE GREAT IRON WAR

Hopebreaker
Lifemaker
Skyshaker
Landquaker
Worldwaker
Hometaker

THE COILHUNTER CHRONICLES

Coilhunter
Rustkiller
Dustrunner

HIBERNIAN HOLLOWS

Hibernian Blood
Hibernian Charm

INFINITE STARS

Infinite Waste
Infinite Worlds

A HIBERNIAN HOLLOWS NOVEL

HIBERNIAN CHARM

DEAN F. WILSON

Cover illustration by Imad ud Din

First Edition 2017

ISBN 978-1-909356-20-7

Published by Dioscuri Press
Dublin, Ireland

www.dioscuripress.com
enquiries@dioscuripress.com

"*The world is full of magic things,
patiently waiting for our senses to grow sharper.*"

— W.B. Yeats

In ancient times, the Romans called Ireland *Hibernia*. Much of the magic and mystery of the Emerald Isle has been lost over the years, but those with a second sight can see the secret life, the hidden world, where the line between myth and reality blurs. If you can see that, you've entered the Hibernian Hollows. Getting out is not so easy.

CONTENTS

Chapter

CALLING CARD

She showed up out of the blue. No name. No identity. She was just a child, a girl of six or seven. And she was paralysed, unable to move or talk—unable to tell anyone who or what had done this to her.

The only clue was a small charm bracelet on her left wrist, with all but one of the charms missing. It was like a calling card, but right now no one knew who to call. It would be just another case in the Unexplained Files.

Melanie Rosen spent a lot of time on those cases. Resources were tight in the Occult Investigations Unit—the OIU, or "the Vowels," as it was often called—and the Irish police, An Garda Síochána, didn't like delving too deeply into the strange and unknown. There was a different government agency for that, and people spoke of it in hushed tones, if they even spoke of it at all.

Melanie was given the "dud" cases, the ones that weren't just cold, but getting colder. It was a kind of balance for her hot-headed nature, a way to keep her out of trouble. They could have just sacked her, but then she'd be free to follow her own lines of investigation. They had to keep an eye on her. That was the funny thing about all of this. There were a lot of eyes watching, and not all of them were human.

But this case was different. This was one of the few times where they picked her for her expertise.

"You know charms, right?" Don, head of the OIU, asked. Life hadn't been good to him, but then he hadn't been good to himself either. He was still smoking those same cigars that cracked his skin and yellowed his teeth.

"A bit, yes." She never liked Don, and she never tried to hide her contempt.

"A bit?" he said, looking over his glasses. She was taller than him, so he couldn't look down on her, but this was his way of doing it anyway. And if he couldn't do it with his eyes, he'd do it with his voice. "I thought that was right up your alley, what with you being a gypsy and all."

She cocked her head, letting the brown curls and hair charms roll off her shoulder. "Not really keen on that term."

"Well, get used to it, hun, 'cause it might be one of you lot who's behind all this."

She froze, the fire in her extinguished. "What do you mean?"

"Well, this is the second time we've had someone show up like this, wearing nothing but a charm. We didn't think much of the first. I mean, it was likely just a coincidence. But twice? Nah. We've been in this business too long to not notice the beginning of a pattern."

He held his fist out, face down, and she instinctively cupped her hands in response. She heard the chink as he dropped two charms into her palms. The first was a Hamsa, a protective symbol in the shape of a hand, but bound tightly in cord. The second was a filled-in vesica, designed to suggest a blinded eye, and so protect against the Evil Eye. She didn't really get what they meant in this context. If anything, they hadn't worked to protect the victims.

"Both different," Don said. He wiped his hands on his shirt, as if he didn't like even touching those trinkets. "Now, someone who hasn't been in the police business for thirty years might say: *doesn't that make it look more like coincidence?* And they'd be right. It makes it *look* that way, and that might be the intent."

"Or the perpetrator wants to make a full set," Melanie replied.

"What's that?"

"They were on charm bracelets, right?"

"Yeah. We just kept the charms. Figured the bracelet didn't mean anything."

"But maybe it does. How many attachments were there?"

"Attachments?"

"For charms. How many of them were empty?"

"God knows. Five or six, I think. We'd have to check."

"If I were a betting woman, I'd wager that our man is looking to make a whole set. If there are six attachments total, then we've got four more to go."

"Or woman," Don said.

Melanie raised an eyebrow.

11

"Well, you're all about equality, right? Could be a lass."

"True," she replied. "Whoever it is, we need to find them before they do this to anyone else. It seems to me like the perpetrator is just getting started. Speaking of which, do we even know what the actual cause of the paralysis is?"

"No. The tests have ruled out anything medical."

"Anything scientific," Melanie mused.

"That's why it came to us. They think it might be some kind of magic. Just your cup of tea, eh? Maybe you can read the leaves. It'll keep you and Eckhart busy, anyhow. Probably best for you."

She indulged him with a forced smile.

There was a knock on the door, and one of the junior detectives poked her head through. Melanie hadn't seen this one before. The OIU was a bit like a revolving door. People left just as quickly as they came. Melanie was one of the few who stuck it out, who wanted answers.

"Sorry, sir," the new detective said, "but you asked for updates on the girl."

"Yes?"

"She's regained some movement in her right hand. We think she might be coming out of it."

They rushed down to the medical ward, a facility you only got to see if there were some "anomalies," and boy were there lots of those. They saw the girl in a hospital bed, inside a sealed globe. The entire room was a stark white, the kind of white that wasn't comforting, but rather suggested you were being experimented on. If the girl wasn't paralysed, she might have screamed.

"Why is she in that thing?" Melanie asked, pointing to the globe.

"For her protection," the nearby doctor said. He looked out of his depths here, and seemed to be rifling through papers on a clipboard, more out of habit than intent. He wouldn't find any explanation for the girl's condition there. He'd be better off looking in an old library, under the section marked "Occult."

"And for ours," Don added. He shrugged. "Just in case."

He picked up a microphone from the table. "Can you talk?" he asked.

"She can't talk yet," the doctor said.

"Give me that," Melanie said, tearing the microphone from him. "Sweetheart, we're here to help. We need to know who did this to you. We need to find them before they do it to anyone else. Do you understand?"

The girl couldn't nod yes or no. She couldn't even blink. But she could move her hand. That was about all she could do.

"We need to know who did this to you," Melanie repeated.

The girl pointed, and Melanie almost dropped the microphone. She was pointing at her.

POINTING FINGERS

Melanie had seen a lot of things in her ten years with the OIU, though they'd tried hard to keep her from seeing it all. She took a lot in her stride. She had to. Yet, something about that girl put her on edge. It could've just been a harmless gesture, but in Melanie's world, most things had a meaning. She didn't like what this one implied.

"She pointed at me," Melanie told her police partner, Toby Eckhart. He was a bit more than just a colleague, a bit of a consort, a confidante. If he'd had his way, he might've been even more.

Eckhart tutted. "No, she didn't."

"I swear to God, Eckhart, she did."

"You're reading into things, Mel. She can barely move a finger. She was probably just … I don't know, stretchin' or something. Or she was pointing at the door. Or the wall. Or anywhere. You can't make a case with something like this."

Eckhart was a sceptic, which was saying something when it came to all the occult phenomena they experienced in the Vowels. While some jumped at the thought of a tap on the wall being the sign of a ghost, he was always first to attribute it to some logical cause. He didn't quite gel with many of the other detectives because of that. Many joined the OIU because they wanted to believe. Melanie already believed. She wanted to fix things.

"I don't know why I told you, anyway," Melanie said.

Eckhart grinned. "Because you love me?"

"Now who's reading into things?"

"Hey, what's a partner for? You'd be lost here without me. You wouldn't want to be Don's partner, would you?"

Melanie laughed. "Like that would ever happen. He's had it in for me ever since I joined. Moved me twice. Gave me dud case after dud case. Christ, he gave me this one with the girl." She paused, waiting for Eckhart to crack a smile and point with both index fingers to himself. "Yeah, and he gave me you."

"So not all bad then."

"Heh."

There was a pause, one of those awkward ones that happened so often between them. Those days should have been long gone now. They were on the same team for two years now, and sometimes it still felt like they just got saddled with one another last week.

"So, you're dropping this whole thing about the girl pointing at you, right?"

"Right," Melanie said reluctantly. She knew she probably should. Hell, she should probably drop the whole case and go back to ticking boxes. But the way that girl looked at her—like she'd seen her before. A shiver wormed its way up Melanie's spine.

"You're not gonna drop it, are you?" Eckhart asked, running his hand through his hair.

"No, probably not."

Eckhart rolled his eyes. "You're too predictable."

"And you're not?"

"Hey, I'm as spontaneous and surprising as they come."

Melanie laughed. "Yeah, I'll believe that when I see it."

The laughter died down, letting the awkward silence emerge again. They glanced at each other and gave those forced smiles. It wasn't so bad before he proposed, before he tried to make them partners in a different sense. He took rejection like a champ, didn't make a fuss about it, but it still felt weird since then. Some things just couldn't be unsaid.

"So," he said, piercing the silence. "Where do we start?"

Melanie paced around the room. "We don't have a lot to go on."

"What *do* we have?"

"Two victims, and two charms."

"Two?"

"Yeah."

"Well, let's go visit number one then," Eckhart suggested.

"He's dead."

Eckhart shrugged. "We work in the Vowels, Mel. Death hasn't stopped us before."

THE ORIGINAL VICTIM

"So, where is our … uh, original victim?" Eckhart asked.

Melanie bit her lip. She knew he wasn't going to like this. "Downstairs." That could have been anywhere, of course, but in the OIU, "downstairs" only meant one thing.

"We're not seriously going *there*, are we?"

"Why not?"

"That's where they … do experiments."

"That's only a rumour."

Eckhart raised an eyebrow. "Is it?"

"It doesn't matter what they do. That's where our clue is."

"Our person, you mean."

"To be honest, Eckhart, I'm not sure he's much of anything any more, or won't be for long."

"I guess we better get moving then."

They headed downstairs, using the lift. You had to have a special pass for this, and Don gave it to Melanie with glee. Perhaps he thought she could get up to less trouble down there. She knew all too well he'd be wrong.

The lift shook as it descended. It seemed an awfully long way, like going to Hell. The numbers of the floors no longer registered. They stood silent, staring at the sealed door until it chugged to a halt. A friendly chime preceded the doors opening. The noise was at odds with the other, stranger sounds in the distance, muffled by concrete and steel.

"The Bowels of the Vowels," Eckhart mused. He said it a little quieter. You said everything quieter down here. "You're lucky I hate doing paperwork."

"We all do."

"Well, then you're lucky I hate it more than the thought of this place."

Eckhart might have been the sceptic, but he wasn't sceptical about what they did down here. Melanie couldn't say much to disprove the rumours. Any answer she had was quashed by a cry of pain from behind some sealed metal door with frosted windows.

A doctor was waiting for them at the end of the corridor. "Doctor" might have been a loose term. Melanie had seen all sorts go downstairs: researchers, politicians, magicians, and even monsters. They preferred different names, of course. Vampires, werewolves, fey. To Melanie, most of them were monsters all the same. Some of them were even human.

"Patient 109-3A?" the doctor inquired.

"The paralysis victim," Melanie said.

"That's the one. Follow me."

They followed him through the maze of tunnels. They stopped being corridors after a while, shifting to metal tubes. Some of them were encrusted with seals and talismans, glowing faintly.

"To protect us," the doctor said, when he noticed their stares.

"From what?" Eckhart asked. Melanie caught his gaze, and knew he wished he hadn't asked at all.

"You don't want to know."

The doctor led them to one of the generic sealed rooms, drawing a symbol on a keypad, which let them in. They were immediately taken aback by the sight of a naked man suspended in a glass tube, completely frozen and wide-eyed.

"Jesus," Eckhart blurted.

"Is he … still alive?" Melanie asked. Don had told her the first guy was dead. He might as well have been.

"Barely," the doctor said. "He has some vitals. He seems to fade in and out of consciousness. He was able to twitch his nose when he first came in. No longer."

Melanie circled around the glass tube. "Have you been able to identify a cause?"

"No. This doesn't match any of the usual causes for something like this."

Eckhart grimaced. "The usual causes?"

"Poisons, diseases, exposure to certain paranormal influences, and so forth. There's no obvious sign of anything, no crackle of energy to suggest magic, no markings to suggest a foreign invasion of any kind. It just … is."

Eckhart sauntered up to the glass, pressing his face close to it, close enough that he could stare into the man's panicked eyes.

"God," he said. "I can only imagine what he must be going through. Can't you, like, do something?"

"Without a cause, we can't cure him."

"No. I mean … like, maybe … I don't know, put him out of his misery."

"That would be unethical."

"And *this* isn't?" Eckhart gestured to the tube.

"He's valuable research."

"He's a human being, for Christ's sake."

"And not everyone in this world is," the doctor said. "The sooner we know our weaknesses, the sooner we can devise ways to plug those gaps. We don't want to be caught on the back foot when it comes to these … others."

"You're right there," Eckhart said, "but couldn't you at least get him some clothes?"

"We can't have any interferences."

"Well," Melanie said, "thanks for your time."

The doctor didn't even give a nod. He'd spent so much time down there with his experiments, where he didn't need his manners, that he'd largely forgotten how to interact with others. He was there to observe, to test, to document. Maybe he was there to torture too.

Eckhart skipped out after Melanie as quickly as he could, putting his arm around her shoulder. "Glad we're out of there," he said with a shudder. "I told you they do weird stuff."

"Everyone does weird stuff nowadays, it seems."

"Not everyone. Anyway, did you actually learn anything from that?"

"Yes," Melanie said as they got to the lift. "I learned what happens when this paralysis kicks in fully. We've got to stop the perpetrator before they do it to anyone else."

LIKELY SUSPECTS

Their first port of call was the esoteric bar known as the Monolith. It was bang smack in the City Centre, and yet it was largely unknown to most people. That was because it was the favourite haunt of another group, some of which weren't even people at all.

Melanie pushed the front doors open, and the usual din fell to a quiet whisper. There was no doubt who they were whispering about. If there was, all those bladed eyes removed it entirely.

"No, no, no," the owner, Oscar Elsey, said. He shimmied up to them, shaking his hips as he walked. If it wasn't for his muscular frame, he would have seemed quite fey. Yet that was the funny thing about this other world so many lived in: fey often meant something else.

"We're just here for a drink," Melanie said.

Oscar cackled. "What, the copshop got none?"

Eckhart shuffled up to him, bearing his chest. He looked remarkably small next to Oscar, but then everyone did. "We heard you're the best around."

Oscar smiled. "You talkin' about me or the bar?"

Eckhart shrugged.

"He doesn't know what he's talking about," Melanie said, pushing in between them. "Why don't you get us a drink, Oscar? You know what I like."

"Yeah," Oscar said with a scoff. "You like to cause trouble. I can't let you in, Melanie. You spook the customers."

"She spooks *them*?" Eckhart asked. "Isn't *spook* slang for one of you lot?"

"Isn't it slang for one of you?" Oscar replied. "I don't need spies here."

"We're not spies," Melanie said.

"Well, the Vowels ain't no normal Garda unit, is it?"

Eckhart grinned. "More normal than you."

"Boys," Melanie said. "Can't we just settle this over a cocktail? I've had a hard day. I just want a quiet drink."

Oscar grumbled, leading them to the bar. "You think you've had a hard day? Try keeping the Kavanaghs and O'Neills away from each other's throats."

"We've tried," Melanie said, pulling up a stool.

"Yeah, best steer clear of them, Melanie."

"I've told her that before," Eckhart said. "Don't mess with the vampires."

Oscar let out a low purr at him. "Don't mess with the werewolves either."

"Well," Eckhart said. "Wait till the New Moon first."

"Have you heard anything strange lately?"

Melanie asked.

Oscar couldn't contain his smile. "Strange? Girl, my whole world is strange!"

"You said it," Eckhart remarked, raising his glass.

"Yeah, I know, Oscar, but … stranger than normal."

"Well, there were these rumours about a new warlock in town. Malik Oaken"

"Oh?"

Oscar leant in close, and seemed about to spill the beans on the latest gossip, but then he halted and snapped his jaw shut. "This isn't official police business, is it?"

"Not official," she said.

He grumbled again. "Well, you didn't hear this from me, but it's been said he's wanted in Amsterdam for a string of occult crimes. Apparently he set up a coven to lure young women in, and no one's seen them since. All the covens here have their members on high alert."

"Why don't they, uh, do some magic against him?" Eckhart asked.

"Because he's got his own. Defences up the wazoo."

Eckhart forced a straight face. "Up there, huh?"

"Do you have any details on him?" Melanie asked.

"Here," Oscar said, pulling a poster from the wall. It showed the faces of a dozen people the bartenders were not to serve. He tapped his finger at Malik's image, with his high brow and long, black hair. He looked like he came from a bygone era. As far as Melanie was concerned, he should have stayed there.

"He looks grim."

"He *is* grim," Oscar said.

"How did you get this photo?"

"Let's just say, a little faerie took it for me."

"And all I've got are little birdies," Eckhart said. "I could do with an upgrade."

Melanie was about to hand the poster back when she saw her and Eckhart's faces on the bottom row. She scoffed.

"Hey, girl, I told you you weren't supposed to be in here," Oscar said.

"We're not *that* bad, are we?"

"It depends who you ask."

"I'm asking you."

"Well, I like you, personally."

"And what about me?" Eckhart asked.

"What about you?"

"Sheesh."

Melanie tapped her hand forcefully at Malik's image, as if she could crush him from afar. They turned their attention back to the warlock.

"Is he known for anything like … paralysis?" Melanie asked.

Oscar stopped mid top-up of her glass. "Oh. That."

"So, you heard."

"We *all* heard about that."

"And?"

"It's a mystery."

"But this warlock," Melanie said. "Is he known for that?"

"He's known for all sorts, but I hadn't heard of

this before."

"When did he arrive in Dublin?"

Oscar scrunched his mouth. "I don't know. About two weeks ago."

Melanie looked at Eckhart.

"Coincidence?" he said.

"Not in this world."

"Let me guess," Oscar said. "The paralysis victims only started showing up in the last two weeks."

Eckhart gave him the finger gun, with a double tick of his tongue. "You shoulda been a detective."

Oscar groaned. "Not for a million bucks. You haven't heard of this warlock, have you? One of the other crimes he's wanted for is the murder of dozens of police across Europe. There's nothing he hates more."

Eckhart bit his lip, then turned to Melanie. "Maybe we should ask for those dud cases back. I didn't really *mind* the paperwork."

BACK-ALLEY MAGIC

They had a name, and a face to go with it, but they knew they couldn't rely on that photo. Some warlocks could change their appearance. He could look like anyone. Melanie pushed down the thought that he might even look like her.

They scoured some of the magical hotspots of Dublin City Centre, all those back alleys behind the occult bookshops, meditation centres, and nondescript buildings that belonged to various secret societies. Maybe some of the people who frequented those places thought they were being discreet, but the OIU had most of those locations mapped out. They were patrolled, even if not everyone knew it.

They were getting nowhere with their inquiries until they went to the street behind House of Stars, an occult bookshop not far from Central Bank. A few covens met there for moot and lectures, and some of their members hung out outside, with all those stragglers who couldn't get in. It was the place to be, like waiting outside a concert hall.

Melanie flashed her badge. A few scarpered at the

sight of it. "Hello, boys and girls." Some rolled their eyes at her. "I'm wondering if any of you can help us."

"No one can help *you*," one of the teen girls said, eyeing her up and down as if her outfit was an affront to the gods. Maybe it was. It was certainly an affront to the gods of the OIU. It was like everything about Melanie, a bit of a mish-mash, a bit of a culture clash. Some of it said authority, but some of it said rebel.

"That's too bad," Melanie said. "Because helping me might help you."

"How?"

"We're looking for a warlock."

"We just call them witches, hun," an older woman said.

"I call him Malik Oaken."

All those sniggers stopped abruptly. More of the crowd started to part. Even the cocky teen turned away.

"We don't want anything to do with him," the old woman said.

"Good. I want him locked up. So, maybe you can help me find him."

The old woman's face grew pale. "He'll know," she whispered.

Melanie gestured to the teen. "This your daughter?"

"My niece."

"You know what he does to girls like her?"

The woman sighed and shook her head. "Yes."

"Then help me."

The woman sighed again. "He'll kill me."

"He'll kill a lot of people if we don't catch him,"

Eckhart said.

She eyed the two of them, then glanced at the teen girl, who didn't look half as cocky as she did before. There wasn't a magic-user in Ireland who hadn't heard of Malik Oaken by now. He was one of the rock stars of the occult world, a rock star you didn't want to meet.

"He's at Ballyboden Bastion."

"The O'Neills' place?"

"It's not theirs now. There aren't many of them left."

"What's he doing there?"

"Goddess knows. I heard rumours he's trying to raise some of the slain vampires."

"As if we need more of those," Eckhart said.

"Right, well, thanks for your help," Melanie said.

"You're not going there alone, are you?" the old woman asked.

Melanie looked at Eckhart. "Not alone."

"He'll kill you."

Eckhart raised an eyebrow. "Eh, maybe I'll wait in the car."

"You need a powerful magician to take him on," the old woman said.

Melanie smiled. "I know a guy."

FRIENDS IN HIGH PLACES

It didn't take them long to get to the National Library of Ireland. It was after hours now, so it was closed, or so it seemed to the public. They waited outside in their car. Everyone had their favourite haunt. This was one of Melanie's.

"Are you sure about this?" Eckhart asked.

"As sure as I've ever been," Melanie responded.

"So, not very then."

Melanie smiled. "Not very."

"What if he says no?"

"Then he says no."

"Yeah, but … we're not really going after this warlock by ourselves, are we? I mean, what are we supposed to do? He can probably teleport out of cuffs."

"Then our friend better say yes."

"Hey, he's *your* friend, not mine."

At that moment, the glass door of the Manuscripts Department opened, and out came a tall, thin man with greying hair. He locked up, glanced around, then put up his umbrella, even though it wasn't raining.

He skipped down the steps and started walking down Kildare Street.

Eckhart pressed gently on the accelerator, cruising along behind him. Then the clouds parted like waves and the rain cascaded down.

"Get him to pick the numbers for the lotto," Eckhart suggested.

Then, just as suddenly, they lost him. Within the fraction of a second it took to blink, he was gone, as if they'd fallen asleep and he'd vanished around the corner. There was a sense of cloudiness in their minds, as if the sky had fallen there too.

"I don't gamble," a voice came from the seat behind them.

They jumped, finding the librarian sitting in the back seat, cross-legged, dangling the handle of his quite dry umbrella over his outstretched index finger.

"Jesus!" Eckhart exclaimed.

"No," Mr. Constant said, "not quite, but he was a magician in his own right."

"You shouldn't do that," Melanie said, "sneaking up on people."

Mr. Constant gave the slightest of smiles beneath his moustache. "And what exactly were *you* doing, Melanie Miri Rosen?"

Eckhart raised his eyebrows. "Your full name," he whispered, as if to say: *Now you're in trouble*.

"And what about you?" the magician asked him. "Toby Matthew Eckhart."

"Christ, how'd you know that?"

"It's on your badge," Mr. Constant said, holding it up.

"I won't even ask how you got that."

"From your pocket, of course."

"Ernest," Melanie said.

"Yes?"

"You might be wondering why we're here."

"I'm wondering why you haven't told me yet."

"We're looking for a warlock."

Mr. Constant furrowed his brow. "Well, don't look at *me*."

"No. There's someone new in town. Goes by the name Malik—"

"Oaken," Mr. Constant interjected. "Malik Oaken."

"You know him?"

"Yes. He was refused entry into the Order."

"The Golden Dawn?"

"The very same."

"We need to catch him," Melanie urged.

"*We* don't need to do anything. That's outside my remit."

"But surely you want him caught as much as we do."

"Surely, indeed, but I'm not interested in magical wars. That's not what the Order is about."

"I'm not asking you to do this on official business. Can you do it … as a friend?"

Mr. Constant grumbled, stabbing the end of the umbrella into the floor. "*Fine*," he said. "I'm doing this for your grandmother Tsura though. And all of this is off the record. I don't want to find my name in some police report." He held up his index finger. "Not again."

"I'll write in magic ink," Eckhart said with a chuckle.

Mr. Constant was not amused. "If we're not careful with Malik, you'll be writing it in blood."

OUTSIDE THE
BROKEN FORTRESS

Ballyboden Bastion was in Rathfarnham, at the edge of the Dublin mountains, built by the O'Neill vampires to spy on the nearby Umbra Montis mansion owned by the rival Kavanagh vampire clan. Since the recent collapse of the O'Neill family, the Bastion had largely been abandoned, but no one dared take it over, for fear that somehow they might offend the O'Neills even from beyond the grave. Malik Oaken didn't seem to have those fears. He went anywhere he pleased.

"It still looks unfinished," Melanie said as they drew up to those castle walls.

"This is where they bred their army," Mr. Constant said.

"One for the history books, huh?" Eckhart said, nudging him.

"You won't find any of this in the public parts of the National Library," the magician replied. "These are the annals of the hidden life, the secret world."

"The Hollows," Eckhart said.

"What's that?"

"The Hibernian Hollows, I've heard it called."

Mr. Constant fidgeted with his moustache. "Yes, I suppose you could call it that."

"How do we get in?" Melanie asked. She was already at the boot of the car, pulling out ropes and tools.

"Through the front door," Mr. Constant said. "That's often a good place to start."

"Oh. I thought it'd be barred."

"Fear and rumour is this fortress' defence now."

"Well, it's working," Eckhart said.

"So, I guess I won't need these," Melanie said, casting the items back into the boot.

"Have you got stakes?"

"Yes. Will we need them?"

"This is vampire territory, Melanie. You'll need them if you need your life."

"I thought they were dead," Eckhart said. "The O'Neills, that is."

"They were already dead," the magician replied. "Never be surprised if they can die a few times more. Bring those stakes."

"We have stake-loaded guns," Eckhart suggested.

"Even better then."

"And what about the warlock?"

Mr. Constant pursed his lips. "Bring everything you've got."

THE LAND OF THE DEAD

When they had assembled their supplies, feeling overburdened by them, and noting that Mr. Constant seemed to have nothing at all, they carefully stalked up to the gigantic gate of the castle's outer wall. It was a new building, but it looked ancient. Some of it was purposely aged. Other parts were moved from other sites of antiquity.

The portcullis was up, with its bladed edges dangling above their heads. Mr. Constant strolled through leisurely, Melanie charged after, and Eckhart darted along behind her, ducking low.

"I guess he's expecting visitors," Eckhart quipped.

Mr. Constant gave him a silent glare.

They walked into the courtyard, eyeing the circular pits on either side, where some of the vampires were birthed, and where others were forced to fight for their first meal. Tradition was big in the vampire world, and the first bite was as sacred to them as holy communion.

There were rumours that people mad enough to walk the mountains were captured and dragged here.

Melanie had fought for an investigation for weeks, but it was always refused. Don had said, "Keep to your own, and let them keep to theirs. Let the Kavanaghs sort them out." It was always the same in the OIU. That wasn't what it was supposed to be like, as far as Melanie was concerned. They should've been out there doing something. Like this. Mr. Constant didn't need to worry about a police report, because Melanie knew she couldn't file it anyway, not without risking her badge. She'd spent most of the last decade risking that.

"Now that I think about it," Eckhart said, "maybe we should've waited till day?"

"Fear not the dark," Mr. Constant said. He flicked the fingers of his right hand, producing a faint glow. "Not when you bring the light."

They carried on, towards the keep. That door was broken apart, as if the castle had been raided. It was possible that the Kavanaghs had cleared the place out after the recent vampire war, but Malik could have filled it up again. The Kavanaghs could've done that too. Melanie had met their leader, Rua. She seemed like she obeyed some kind of unwritten vampire rules, but she was still a vampire all the same.

"What if he already knows we're coming?" Melanie whispered.

"What if he already knows we're here?" Eckhart added.

"Stay close to me," Mr. Constant said. "While in my sphere, you won't be seen or heard. You don't even need to whisper. As far as the outer world is concerned, none of us exist."

"I've got mixed feelings about that," Eckhart said. "Kinda like existing."

Suddenly they heard a stir on the landing above. The shimmer of cloud around them faded. They looked up, aghast, spotting Malik Oaken standing there, holding aloft a staff crowned with fire. His eyes looked fierce.

"Why pretend, Ernie?" Malik shouted down. "Let's make you not exist at all."

BLINK

By the look of strain on Mr. Constant's face, it took almost everything he had to shield them from the fireball that came their way. He'd been caught off guard, and they were lucky he was as experienced as he was or they wouldn't have survived the blast at all.

He grabbed the two of them and shouted some strange, unintelligible words, which seemed to roll off his tongue and then out to the ends of the universe, growing vaster as they went. Then, in the blink of an eye, Melanie found herself alone on one of the rampart walls, far away from the battle. She could only imagine, and hope, that Eckhart was in a similar position elsewhere. She had no idea where Mr. Constant was, but presumed he had teleported away too, so that he could better prepare himself for Malik's assault.

Melanie ducked low, peeping through the castle's crenellations. She could see periodic bursts of light and flame coming from the keep, followed by bouts of intense darkness, which seemed to suck everything towards that location like a black hole.

She scurried along the outer wall, keeping low. She wasn't exactly sure why she was hiding, if the battle was that far off, but she knew enough about magicians and their farsight. For all her boom and bluster, she knew when to lay low.

She arrived at a door leading to one of the higher levels of the keep. She tried the handle, but it was sealed tight. She was just ready to fire her pistol at the lock when the door rocked and came off its hinges. The vestiges of a fireball came through, and she managed to hide behind the wall just in time.

From there, she could hear Malik's heavy boots climbing the stone steps inside. More than that, she could feel his presence, strong and foreboding. He made no attempt to hide, not like Mr. Constant, not like the rest of them. He wanted them to know he was coming.

"You didn't want to teach me, huh, Ernie?" Malik shouted up the stairs. Melanie hadn't seen him, but she guessed Mr. Constant must have gone that way.

"Maybe I should've taught you," Malik added, sending another blast through the ceiling.

Melanie felt her chest rise and fall like an earthquake. She felt that horrible sinking in her gut when you were this close to death. She felt it even more knowing that she'd brought Eckhart and Mr. Constant into this. She worried that maybe her magician wasn't as ready for this as she thought.

She crept out after Malik, waiting until even his shadow had passed upstairs. There were rumours that some magicians could give their shadows eyes. Ever since discovering this other world that lived beneath and beyond our current one, Melanie didn't know what was fact or fiction any more. Often it was a little bit of both.

She held her pistol close. That was her wand. A magician might have flung bolts and fireballs, but she flung bullets. You could have all the magic in the world, but metal and flesh mixed like alchemy, producing death.

She stalked those steps, trying not to let her heels clip the ground too harshly, trying not to let her breath wheeze too noisily. The air crackled with energy. She could feel her gun buzz with it, like a conductor. Everything was a haze, everything except her desire to catch Malik. She didn't mind catching him with lead either. Death was as good a prison as any.

She reached the flat roof of the keep, where she peeped out to see Malik and Ernest squaring off, staff and wand at the ready. Ernest held a glowing copper rod, and for all his might and mystery, he seemed outmatched by Malik in almost all regards.

"Under the night sky," Malik crooned.

"Where there are a billion lights," Mr. Constant replied.

They circled each other, forcing Melanie to duck low to avoid being seen.

"Well, Ernie. One of them is about to go out."

"You can only hide the light with darkness. You cannot extinguish it."

"We'll see about that," Malik said. "But maybe you don't really care about your life. What about the other two? Don't think I didn't see them through your haze."

Mr. Constant glared at him. "This is between you and I."

"*This* is, but I've got a little something else for them."

The look of horror on Mr. Constant's face must have been soul-destroying, but Melanie didn't see it. Her eyes were fixed on the stairs below her, where she could see the shadows of several figures approaching, and hear the snarls that came with them. She knew in her heart, and maybe even in her soul, that they were vampires.

A BITE BELOW

The first vampire came around the corner, leaning low, its claws outstretching like a prancing predator. It caught the scent and sight of Melanie, snarling as it sprang.

But she was ready for it, though barely. She kicked with all her might, sending it sprawling down the steps. She was lucky it was weak, that it had woken from magic and not from the deep, regenerating rest that strengthened its kin.

She fumbled for her supplies, even as the next one came. It leapt out of the way of the falling vampire, casting itself onto the wall, where it clung and crawled like a spider. It advanced towards her, its eyes red with hate, its fangs bared with hunger.

She barely managed to pull a vial of holy water from her belt before the vampire lunged at her, swatting the glass away. It tumbled down the steps, smashing below, where several other vampires howled at the vaporous explosion.

Melanie raised her gun, firing at the vampire, even though she knew she could not kill it like that.

She emptied the barrel, tearing a cry of pain from the creature, but the wounds only slowed it down. They didn't stop it.

She reached again for her backpack, but the vampire was on her, slashing at her face with its vicious claws. She screamed and scrambled, bashing with her hands, thrashing with her feet. She managed to roll over in the fray, exposing her backpack, where a large metal cross was on show. The vampire yelped and leapt away, hanging from the ceiling like a frightened cat.

Melanie tried to run up the stairs, but another vampire came from below, seizing her by the ankle. It pulled her down, and she smacked her chin off one of the stone steps. The pain was overwhelming, but the fear was stronger yet. She tried to free herself, tried to shake off that cold, unholy clutch. She could see the moonlight and starlight above, and the blasts of energy as Malik and Mr. Constant battled. Then she could see it all slipping away as the vampire pulled her down the steps, ready for the feast.

THE DARKNESS

Eckhart didn't knew where he'd been teleported to. It looked like a chamber in the basement, dank and dark. There was a steady drip of water in the corner. Far off, he thought he heard the sound of chains. He just hoped it wasn't a dungeon instead.

He held his pistol in his right hand and his crossbow in his left, with a wooden stake primed and ready as ammunition. That way he was good to go against the living or the dead. He wasn't entirely sure which he feared the most.

His eyes took a long time to adjust to the darkness. In his mind, he thought he saw far-off flashes, but there was nothing here but gloom. Mr. Constant might have sent him away from the battle, but down here he felt anything but safe.

"Mel," he whispered. He wondered why she wasn't with him. To him, it didn't make sense to split them up. Then again, maybe against a warlock with area-of-effect attacks, there wasn't any such thing as safety in numbers.

There was no response, only the eternal glare

of the darkness. He never feared the darkness as a child, never jumped at the shadows on the walls. He had a logical mind, even then. Night came with the revolution of the earth. It wasn't sent by phantoms. Yet, here in Ballyboden Bastion, the surety of science dissolved as swiftly as Mr. Constant's shield. Here the darkness seemed to come from something else.

He felt his way along the wall of the chamber until he found a door. It seemed to be jammed, and the wood was waterlogged. He had to put his weapons away just to haul it open. He didn't like having to do that.

He crept along the passageway, following a faint pinprick of light, which must have come from some opening farther ahead. Even the light he couldn't depend on. Down here, that had a different feel too. He'd heard of wisps used by magicians to lure people astray. You couldn't trust anything. You couldn't trust anyone.

Yet he had little choice. The light beckoned. The darkness ushered him on.

He found himself at the bottom of an old spiral stairwell. The steps were cracked and broken. This part seemed much older than the rest. The O'Neills must have built their castle on some ancient ruins. That gave it even greater power. No wonder Malik was drawn there.

He climbed up, squinting as the light grew brighter, until he arrived in a large rectangular chamber, illuminated by several ever-burning lanterns. When his eyes adjusted, he caught his breath, and his heart panged out a warning beat. He was standing right in the middle of a crypt. On either side were dozens of coffins, some propped against the wall, others laid flat on the floor. He didn't need to pry them open to know what was resting inside. He tried not to breathe, not to let anything disturb that tense air. He feared they'd open from the inside.

THE BARBAROUS WORDS

No matter how much Melanie dug her nails into the stone, the steps would not save her. She carved lines down one step, then another. Every granite block she marked was another step closer to her doom. She could feel it. She could feel that cold grasp around her ankle, like the hand of Death.

The vampire pulled her to the floor, then turned her around, until she could see its dark eyes, with that little glimmer of red fire, which might have been a flicker from Hell. Some said you could get lost in those eyes, consumed by the stare. Though this vampire was weak compared to many, she felt the pull, the lure.

But she felt something else. Deep inside the well of her being, beneath the raging voices of her mind and the rampant fears of her heart, she felt some ancient power stretching back for generations. She saw it as a hand grasping another hand, back into antiquity. Some of the hands were faint, some barely visible at all, but the link was there. She saw her own hand at the end of the chain. For a moment, she didn't know what to make of this. She also knew she didn't have a moment to spare.

Instinct drove to her pull one of the charms out from her hair and hold it up to the vampire. She had used it partly as a nod to her past, to her family, and partly—though she didn't like to admit this—just for fashion. She was glad of her vanity now, and gladder she remembered an old verse her grandmother had told her when she gave her this charm. It was in a strange language, and she did not quite know the translation, but when she spoke, she got a sense of its meaning: "Keep me safe from the hands of the wicked."

The vampire heard the words, but did not heed them. It raised its claw and slashed. Melanie closed her eyes, holding the charm aloft, feeling a mix of confidence and fear. Then she heard the vampire scream, and when she looked again she saw that its hand was dashed apart upon some invisible shield, splintering into a thousand pieces, like a hewn rock.

The creature recoiled, and the other vampires that gathered there backed off too. They bore their fangs, spitting and snarling, perhaps uttering some evil curses in whatever language was spoken by demons. Some said they spoke every language, the better to make everyone listen.

Melanie stood up, and made them listen too. She spoke those words again. Some called them the barbarous words, and cautioned that though we might not now understand them, they should never be changed. They were the roots of ancient powers, hidden beneath the many-branching tree of the languages of today. They were the words of creation and destruction, and the vampires trembled before them like mortals before gods.

But Melanie knew she was no god. She knew that what respite this had given her would be altogether brief. This charm was but a token of a greater power, given to her to wield for a fraction of the fleeting lives of man and woman. It was her birthright to wield it, a link to her people, and yet she was reminded of that constant feeling she had: that she had no people, that her mix of Irish and Romani roots just left her wandering between worlds, unsure of where she belonged. That doubt, more than anything, weakened the effect of the charm.

The vampires sensed it too.

IN THE EYE
OF THE STORM

Melanie ran, leaping up several steps at a time, back up towards the roof, back to where Malik and Mr. Constant continued their deadly duel. No sooner had she make those first flurry of steps than the vampires were in chase, even the vampire with one hand, hungry now for revenge as well as blood.

Melanie slung the backpack off, holding it before her as she scaled her way to freedom. She rummaged through with haste, looking for a stake, a cross, some holy water, some sacred symbol, some little thread of life to cling onto. She worked so fast, and her attention was so drawn by the steps ahead and the vampires behind, that she lost her grip on the backpack altogether. It tumbled down behind her, beneath the feet of the approaching vampires, with all its tools and weapons sealed within.

She had no time for sighs or shouts, and barely enough time to catch her fleeting breath. She threw herself up the remaining steps, out onto the roof, where she was almost blinded by a sudden burst of light. She scrambled up, away from the frenzy of claws at her feet, and she was glad the light was blinding, for it stalled the vampires for a moment, who feared it was the light of the sun.

"Go back, Melanie!" Mr. Constant shouted. His voice was strained. His face was drawn. He never looked so taxed before in his life. He had told her previously of some of his trials. She never thought she would live through one. She wasn't certain she would live through it all.

Melanie stepped back, but the vampires were there, blocking the way. Some of them started to crawl up, brazen and emboldened by the blanket of the night. She had no choice. She couldn't go back. She had to press forward, right into the firing line.

She ran again, avoiding a blast from Malik's staff. She stumbled, almost into the path of a stray bolt from Mr. Constant's wand. The vampires came like a flood. If she would drown, she would drown in her own blood.

She pulled another charm from her hair, but in her hurry it slipped from her hands, spinning into the sky. She looked up to it, seeing the flicker of stars in the canopy above, seeing the flicker of fire and light from the magicians on either side. She leapt for the charm, but fell short. It struck the ground and began to roll.

The vampires were close now, ducking low to avoid the barrage of magical missiles sent from side to side.

Melanie reached out to grasp the charm, but

the vampires leapt too. She almost had it, and was readying the words that might turn those fiends to dust, when she felt a monumental force pulling her back. She looked down to see a gigantic astral hand, cast from Mr. Constant's own, yanking her out of the way of the leaping vampires.

The vampires rolled in place, then sprinted back across the roof to where Melanie lay. Mr. Constant still struggled with Malik, who was straining too, but now the magician moved about on the roof with a sudden speed, his left arm held out like a shield, casting a bluish aura around him, and his right hand sending blasts of light towards a vampire here, then a vampire there, each of them exploding into dust in turn.

He reached Melanie, and she felt like she was sucked into a bubble. She could see the faint glow around her, but it was overcome by a steady stream of fire from Malik's staff.

Mr. Constant gasped. "I can't … hold … this … for long!"

They caught each other's gaze, and she knew what he meant to do. He would hold off Malik while she ran, back down the steps, back through the gate, back to the car. It might as well have been back to the desk and paperwork too.

The magician must have seen the fire in her eyes. He knew she would defy him. It required no divination to know that.

Before he could grasp her arm and hold her back, she jumped out of the protective globe and raced across the roof to where the fallen charm lay.

Mr. Constant held Malik's fire, but Melanie drew the warlock's gaze.

She dived, just as Malik started to turn his staff towards her. Her fingers caught the edge of the charm, and she tumbled in place, landing on one knee. She faced the warlock, seeing like a vision the torture he put so many young women through. She heard a hundred women's screams, but this time they came with her own as she spoke aloud an ancient verse.

A pillar of light fell from the heaven, straight down upon Malik, blasting apart his staff and tearing asunder his robes. He was left there, frazzled and shaking, a fragment of his former self. If anyone had seen him then, they would not have feared him.

Mr. Constant wheezed as he fell to his knees, exhausted. Melanie struggled with her own sudden fatigue. She had no idea what had happened, or how. She worked on instinct, like the draw of a gun.

The battle was over, and everyone had lost their energy. Yet, deep inside, Melanie felt a hint of hope. With Malik defeated, there would be no more paralysis victims. They would interrogate him. They would bring him "downstairs." They would get the answers they needed to free that poor girl and man.

Then she jumped as a sound like thunder rang out. She knew that sound. She knew it all too well. There was Eckhart at the top of the steps, pointing his smoking pistol towards Malik. The warlock fell, defenceless. Without his magic, he was just a man. Men could be killed.

DONE AND DUSTED

As Malik collapsed, it seemed like the case was collapsing too. Melanie ran to him, like a mother to a child, but she only wanted him to live because he had the answers to her many questions, because maybe he could undo some of the horrors he had inflicted.

"No," she said, feeling for a pulse. It was there, but it was fleeting.

Malik coughed, spluttering blood. The look of shock on his face was harrowing. Perhaps he came here to seek the secrets of life and death. Perhaps he thought that he would live forever. He had built his own bastion of magical defences, yet a pebble of metal tore it all apart.

"Tell me how to undo it," she whispered to Malik. She could barely summon the strength to talk.

Malik choked. She thought maybe he was trying to reveal his secrets, or maybe he was trying to utter some last words of defiance. He spasmed in place, then grew limp, giving one last sigh as his soul drifted off. Where it went, none there knew.

Eckhart came up next to her, his gun still in hand, pointing down, still smoking.

"Is he … ?"

Melanie looked up at him, biting her lip. She shook her head. "Why?" she asked. "We had him. We had him, Toby."

"Men like him deserve to die," Eckhart said. "What prison would hold him?"

"I don't care about that," she said. "What about the girl?"

Eckhart shrugged. "Did you really think we could save her?"

"I hoped we could."

"He would never have told you how to set her free."

"For his own freedom, he might."

"If there's anything I know, Mel, it's that nothing he said would've helped."

Maybe Eckhart was right, but he had to say that. With the click of a trigger, he had closed their case. It was over. The culprit was dead, and his victims would be joining him. All of Malik's secrets, his techniques, his spells, went with him to the grave.

Mr. Constant helped Melanie to her feet, though he was unsteady on his own. His skin was pale, and his hair was unkempt. He never looked so old before. Normally he looked timeless.

"We did what we could," the magician said. His voice, though weak, was as reassuring as ever, like a tropical island in a stormy sea.

"We did what we set out to do," Eckhart added.

That was true, for them. Malik had to be taken

care of. But for her, she needed answers. She needed a way to set things right. She wasn't sure if it was because of some overriding sense of justice, or if it was because she somehow felt like she was partially to blame. She couldn't get the image of that girl pointing at her out of her head.

She hobbled away, shrugging off Eckhart's hand. Though he meant well, it was no comfort to her. He had stolen her answers. She had gotten nowhere with so many cases. She thought this was finally the one she could solve.

She heard a dull ringing, but could not concentrate on it.

"I'm sorry!" Eckhart shouted over.

The ringing grew, until finally she realised it was her phone. She took it out and answered it absent-mindedly. It was Don. He sounded worried.

"Melanie? I've been tryin' to reach you."

"Oh," was all she could manage.

"You should come back to the station."

"Why?"

"We found another one."

THIRD TIME'S THE CHARM

Melanie and Eckhart rushed back to the station, while Mr. Constant said he'd take care of Malik. There would be no police report. The trio pledged each other to silence. The magician was used to that. Melanie wasn't. All that anyone else would know was that Malik was gone. No one cared enough about him to ask where.

The drive back was full of tense silence, as if their pledge was active then as well. Melanie spotted Eckhart glancing at her from time to time. It seemed like he wanted to talk, to apologise. But there wasn't anything to apologise for. If there was another victim, then maybe Malik wasn't responsible at all.

Don was quieter than usual in the briefing room. He had a report ready for them, with all those boxes nicely ticked. He also had pictures on the wall.

"Another child," he said.

Melanie's heart sank. Ever since she found out as a teenager she couldn't have children of her own, her work became her life, her family. She swore to protect the innocent. There was none more innocent than a child. That's what made this hurt even more, like the culprit had done this to her own. It was like they knew her, like they wanted to get to her. She knew that Eckhart would say that she was just being paranoid.

"He's in the early stages, it seems," Don said.

"The early stages?"

"He's lost all feeling in his arms and legs, but he can still move his head, and—"

"Can he talk?" Melanie interjected.

Don tapped the papers on his desk.

"Can he talk?" Melanie repeated.

"With difficulty, yes."

"I want to talk with him."

"That mightn't be a good idea. He's very confused. We—"

"I *need* to get some answers, Don. We have to ask who did this. If it's not—" She cut herself short, remembering her pledge.

"If it's not?"

"If we don't ask him now, we may lose our chance. What if it spreads? What if ends up like the others?"

"I hate to say it, Melanie," Don said, "but the reports I've got don't account for 'what if'. They say it's pretty much guaranteed he'll fade away. We don't know of any way to reverse this."

"Maybe the perpetrator does."

"What if he doesn't?" Eckhart asked.

"There has to be a way."

"The charm," Eckhart said. "I presume there's one."

Melanie had almost forgotten it. She felt her own

charm uncomfortably in her pocket.

Don pulled an envelope out of a drawer, casting it over to Melanie. She opened it, pulling out a clear plastic bag. Inside was a little golden monkey, covering his ears.

"It seems like it's just random now," Don said. "This looks like it's of Eastern origin."

"It's not random," Melanie said. "These aren't just a calling card. They're protections."

"Hmm?"

"The bound hand. The blinded eye. The covered ears. Whoever's behind this isn't leaving these as breadcrumbs to find him. He doesn't want to be found."

TREMBLE

They gathered outside the patient's room, building up their courage to enter, to put on those brave faces, which covered up the doubtful and exhausted ones beneath.

"Sorry, Mel," Eckhart said. "I think I'll wait outside. I can't see another one like this."

Melanie nodded sympathetically. She didn't want to go in either. She hated to think that it was because she felt she was somehow to blame.

"You always were a softie," Don said to Eckhart. Of course, everyone was soft compared to Don. It was almost like he didn't have a soul. He was all hard shell.

They entered the room where the boy was being kept, strapped to a bed. He struggled with the bonds, and the doctors said no tranquillisers seemed to work. All they really had to do was wait. The paralysis would soon stop him squirming.

"Is he in pain?" Melanie whispered to one of the doctors.

"He doesn't register any physical signs of pain."

"He looks in pain."

"We don't account for the magical signs."

Melanie looked to Don. "Maybe we should have magicians here, not doctors." She didn't care that the doctors could hear her. They didn't seem to be helping the child at all.

"We had all sorts," Don said. "No one's the wiser."

"Can I ask him some questions?"

The doctors nodded begrudgingly and brought her up to the child.

"Hi," Melanie said.

The boy's eyes widened with a look of terror. His struggles became more forceful. He rolled his head back and forth, mumbling frantically.

"What's wrong?" she asked the doctors.

They shrugged, finding nothing in their readings.

"I'm not here to hurt you," Melanie told the child.

Yet, from the boy's reaction, it seemed like he was almost certain she was.

"I'm trying to find who did this to you."

His rambling turned to shrieks. He had lost so much control of his mouth and tongue that none of them could quite make out his words.

"I think that's enough," one of the doctors said. "You're scaring him."

Melanie knew well how the presence of police officers tended to put people on edge, even people with nothing to hide. Yet, this seemed different. She had to bury the thought that it somehow seemed like the boy recognised her. That wouldn't be so bad if he didn't look at her and tremble.

COMFORT

Melanie still shook on her own when they went to a discreet late-night bar known as the Snug. It was so exclusive, you had to have a pass to get in. An ID badge from the Vowels did just fine.

"God," Melanie said, cradling her drink.

"Well, people usually just call me Toby," Eckhart quipped.

Melanie ignored his attempt to lighten the mood. Nothing could lighten it for her.

"Are you okay?" Eckhart asked.

"No. I … that didn't help at all."

"I'm glad I stayed outside."

"I wish I'd done the same, but I had to try."

"Doesn't seem like it made anything clearer."

"I'm not sure," Melanie said. "Maybe it's just paranoia at this stage, but I really did get the impression he'd seen me before."

"He can't have."

"And yet it seemed like he did."

"Maybe on TV?"

"I've never *been* on TV. Don does the public

statements."

"It's probably just your nerves are frazzled. That kid would've probably reacted like that to anyone. To Don. To me."

"But Don was there, and he seemed fine with him."

"Yeah, but Don's probably been in there before."

"It was his first time in that room, same as mine."

"Mel, I really think you're worrying about nothing."

"Am I though? I mean, what if—?"

Eckhart shook his head forcefully. "Don't say that."

"What if it was me?"

"It wasn't you."

"How do you know? *I* don't even know."

"Trust me, Mel, I know it wasn't you. You're not that kind of person. You'd know."

"Yet, at Ballyboden Bastion, I found this hidden power with charms that I didn't know I had. When I got into the moment, it seemed like I almost became a different person. I acted on instinct. I didn't think. What if—?"

"Stop it, Mel. This isn't you."

"But that's my point. What if there's another side of me that I don't even know about? There's so much of my family history I haven't even explored."

Eckhart sighed. "We all have many sides, but I think I know you well enough by now."

"Do you though?"

Eckhart reached over and placed his hand on hers. "I think I do."

She pulled her hand away from him. "Not this again, Toby."

"What?"

"We've been down this road before."

"It's a different road every time, Mel."

"It's the *same* road. It always leads to the same place."

"It doesn't have to."

Melanie rolled her eyes and shook her head. "Toby, you're a nice guy, and on some levels we click, but on this level … we just don't. We've done this all before. You make a move, and I don't reciprocate, and then you get all dejected."

"I don't."

"You do. You get mopey, like a scolded puppy. Can't we just focus on our work?"

"Fine."

"See, you're already doing it."

Eckhart shrugged. "What am I supposed to say? It seems I can't get anything right."

"I'm not asking you to say anything. Just … you know what, let's just call it a night. Today's been stressful enough as it is."

She glanced at a text message on her phone from her ex, and decided it was best to hide it with her hand. She might have been paranoid about the case, but Eckhart was paranoid about her ex. Though they were not together any more, they still had an odd, even close, relationship. She got the feeling Eckhart didn't want them to have any kind at all.

"I'm sorry," Eckhart said. "I didn't mean to make it worse."

"Don't worry about it. I'll see you back at the station tomorrow."

"Bright and early," Eckhart said.

"I don't know about early," Melanie replied. "I need to find some answers. I think I might be up all night."

DIVINATION

Melanie felt bad about leaving Eckhart alone at the bar, but she knew her presence probably wasn't helping. If past experience was anything to go by, he'd drink himself into a stupor and show up to work the next day as if nothing had happened. He might as well have been a magician himself, because he made it seem like he could make his troubles vanish.

She arrived home at close to 3:00 a.m. She was so physically exhausted, she could collapse at any moment, and yet her mind was racing so much she knew she'd never be able to sleep. This was always her problem. She was always restless. She attributed this to her ancestors, travelling from place to place, never settling. It seemed for her that she would never settle either. It wasn't just about bricks and mortar. It was about how you thought and acted, how you felt you fit in. She felt she didn't fit in anywhere. She was just passing through, trying to do some good while she was at it. In a way, she supposed this summed up humanity as a whole. And yet, when she thought of whoever was behind these charm attacks, it clearly seemed that not everyone was trying to do some good.

She pulled the attic ladder down, coughing through the dust. She hadn't been up there in years, not even to get the Christmas decorations down. Her family was so mixed now, they celebrated a bit of everything. Yet she never had time for that. She couldn't even settle in her own home long enough to put up the tree. A pang of regret struck her heart at the inner knowledge that maybe she'd never have a family, that maybe she'd never settle for anyone. By all accounts, Eckhart was a catch. He just wasn't her catch. She wasn't even sure she was fishing at all.

The attic was full of boxes with faint labels. Many were from her grandparents after they died. She hadn't the heart to throw them out, but hadn't the urge to open them either. Some were family heirlooms, links to her Romani roots, but she didn't feel that connected to those roots, so she felt it would be an insult to her family to use them at all.

Buried amongst all the boxes was a set of Tarot cards her grandmother used. It didn't take long to find them. They almost called to her, even though they were just card and ink. It was a very old deck, well over a century old, and the images were slightly faded. They reminded her of the photographs of her grandparents. The energy of her grandmother was still on them.

She took them downstairs and laid out the cards on her coffee table. She paused, looking up and saying a little silent prayer to the dead. She wasn't entirely sure she should even be using these. Her grandmother had taught her how, though her memory of it was fuzzy, but it seemed more like a game to her as a child. Now everything was very real.

She picked a card as the significator, representing her in the situation. This was drawn from the court cards. She picked the Knave of Wands, feeling it matched who she was. It was a young, feminine figure with a fiery, unyielding temperament. She almost didn't like seeing it. It was like looking in a mirror. For something so crude and simple, it was too perfect a match.

She shuffled the deck, reciting a verse in her head that her grandmother made her memorise. It was again in that foreign tongue that no linguist seemed to know anything about. She wasn't sure it meant anything or all, or if it was just to occupy her mind to ensure she didn't influence the reading.

She dealt the cards out in the spread she was taught by her grandmother, which had become known by the quaint moniker "the gypsy method." Mr. Constant had remarked to her before that examples of it, with that very label, were found even in the National Library of Ireland, dating back over a hundred years. She was sworn to secrecy regarding the specific method, and so did not dwell too much even on the form of the spread, lest she inadvertently reveal something even in her sleep. Some called that superstition, but she'd seen enough of the secret world not to disregard the warnings.

She tried not to read anything into the cards as they were laid out, despite momentary gasps of breath as she saw The Tower card, symbolic of destruction, and The Devil card, symbolic of a binding force. By the end of it, the final card, directly opposing her own, was the Knight of Swords. She had been taught to regard all court cards as potential people in the situation, and there were only two, her as the Knave of Wands, and whoever was the Knight of Swords. In a literal reading, it could represent a fair-haired man in his prime, an intellectual. That wasn't a total surprise. The culprit of the crimes had likely studied magic in some depth, and was clearly cunning. A more symbolic reading suggested she would have to use her own wit to cut through the web surrounding the situation.

She glanced over the cards, noticing The Lovers at the point of intersection, the turning point of the event. It might have suggested literal lovers or it could have pointed out a sense of division, of the dual nature of the self. Melanie certainly felt divided. She almost felt like she had lost control on the roof of Ballyboden Bastion. It made her fear even more that maybe she really was behind it all.

She gathered up the cards in various piles, sorting them out in a pre-determined order by the system of rules her grandmother had taught her. This was a more complex reading, delving deeper into the situation, helping her gain some clarity. If anything, it would answer once and for all where she fit into all of this.

The answer was both a relief and a worry. Her card came out in a different place and was not counted in the final reading, suggesting her role was a supporting one, that she was a circling issue, not the driving force. In the centre, though, was the Knight of Swords, seeming to almost orchestrate the cards in the order of his choosing, like a conductor. And there, yet again, was The Lovers, but now it was set directly between the Knave of Wands and the Knight of Swords.

She wished her grandmother was there to give her insight. She was too close to the situation. She wasn't entirely sure she could rely on this at all. Yet, if she could—and her gut told her it was so—then the man behind these crimes was much closer to home.

BROODING

Melanie tried to sleep that night, but she couldn't. She tossed and turned. If anything, that was the symbol of her life. They could have made a Tarot card just for it. The Restless.

The Knight of Swords rode through her mind, slashing as he went, using his shield and armour to hide his identity. Maybe it wasn't even a man at all, as Don had said from the beginning, though she got the impression it was. She wasn't sure if that was instinct or bias.

She tried to doze, but the Knight rode on. He wasn't a knight in shining armour. He was a false knight, with no chivalry or code of honour. Or maybe he had his own twisted form of one. Maybe he thought he was somehow saving his damsel in distress. Melanie was no damsel, but she felt very distressed.

Her mind wandered to her ex. She didn't like the thought of it, but The Lovers card made her go there. Stephen was a nice guy by all accounts, but he wanted to settle in a farm in the country. That wasn't the life for her at all. He dabbled in magic, after she introduced him to this other world of hers, and seemed to take a liking to it, though he never did more than dabble. She warned him about messing with stuff he wasn't ready for, or disrespecting it in the process. That was another of the reasons things just didn't work out between them. And yet, for all of that, they kept in touch. He called her weekly to catch up on things, and they met up monthly too. Eckhart called him "your ex-stalker," and he had warned her off Stephen when they first met. She thought maybe she should have heeded his advice.

NO REST
FOR THE WICKED

Just when Melanie was starting to doze off, she heard a ringing. She instinctively hammered her fist at the bedside locker, but the sound didn't die down. Then she realised it wasn't her alarm clock at all. It was her phone.

She hauled herself up just enough to grab her phone from the table and slump back down into her pillow.

"Yeah?" she said with a yawn.

"There's been another one," Eckhart replied.

Suddenly she felt frightfully awake. She sat up. "What? This soon?"

"Yeah, I wasn't expecting it myself. Half of us are already in at the station."

"I'm on my way," Melanie groaned.

"And Mel, about last night—"

"Forget it. We've got more important stuff to worry about."

Melanie hung up and started getting dressed,

fumbling about for her shoes, leaving her shirt half-unbuttoned. Her hair was a mess, but then it always looked a little frayed. She tried to tidy it up a little, noticing the charms in the mirror. She'd never thought about them so much before.

What does it mean? she asked herself. Her mind drifted back to the Knight of Swords. *What are you trying to achieve?* She'd been warned before about trying too hard to understand the mind of a murderer, but she had to keep on pressing, had to keep on digging. She'd dug herself a lot of holes over the years, upset a lot of people.

Her phone rang again and she answered it without looking at the name.

"I said I'm on my way."

"Hey melon. On your way where?"

It was Stephen. She could hear him puffing away on his cigar. That was another reason things didn't work out. Melanie couldn't stand the stench.

On any other morning, she would have blurted into tales about her day. She would have even told him about the case, about the paralysis victims. Not today. Today, at the mere thought of the Knight of Swords, Stephen called. Melanie could barely give a response at all.

"Are you still there?"

"Yeah."

"What's up? Is something wrong?"

"I can't talk right now."

She hung up, taking a moment to catch her breath. She could talk just fine. She just couldn't talk to him.

INVOKING SILENCE

The fourth victim was a woman in her thirties. She could still move her arms and legs, but her entire face had seized up. Her eyes were clenched tight and her jaw was rigid. It was lucky she could even breathe.

"I'm not going in this time," Melanie said.

"Well, I'm not going in after what you said happened last time," Eckhart replied.

"Jesus," Don said. "You're a bunch of pansies, yous are."

Don went inside, tutting loudly as we went.

Eckhart glanced at Melanie and back to the glass, then back to her again.

"Are you okay?" Eckhart asked.

"Yeah, why?"

"You look a little … frazzled."

"I got a call."

"Oh." Eckhart paused. "From *him*."

"How did you know?"

"It's always him. Didn't I tell you he's a stalker?"

"I hate to think it, Toby, but … you might be right."

"Whatever he is, he's not good for you."

Melanie didn't say it aloud, but she thought it: *I'm not sure he's good for anyone.*

They returned their gaze to the glass, watching as Don calmed the woman down and got her to write something on a notepad. Melanie wanted to go in now and ask her questions, but she fought back the urge. She didn't want to panic her again.

"Do you want me to do it?" Eckhart asked.

"Can you?"

"I don't want to, but … for you, sure."

"Thanks, Toby. You know what to ask."

Toby went inside, joining Don at the woman's bedside. He whispered to the boss, then took over with the pen and paper. Melanie couldn't hear what he was asking, and she paced frantically back and forth outside, biting her knuckles as she went. She was no telepath, but still she urged Eckhart to ask who did this, how they did it, how they knew her, how they got away.

In time, Eckhart came back out with the notepad in hand. Don stayed for a moment, issuing false reassurances to the woman. No one could promise her it would be all right, but Don did it anyway. He never had a problem with lying.

"Well," Eckhart said. "That wasn't pretty."

"What did you get?" Melanie asked.

"Here." He handed her the notepad.

Melanie scoured the text, which was difficult to decipher. "What does it mean?"

"I don't know, to be honest."

"She mentions a man and a woman. Are we

looking for two people?"

"The way this is going, Mel, we could be looking for an army."

"But the man," Mel said. She tried to look for any identifying features. The account didn't give much in the way of details.

"This is a bit generic to go on," Eckhart said. "We'd really want to get an artist in, but the trouble is she can't see. It seems we're back to square one."

Melanie sighed. "I'm not sure we're even at square one any more. It's more like zero."

Don came out, carrying a plastic bag.

"Whoever this joker is," he said, "it seems he went to a gift shop."

He held up the bag.

"What is it?" Eckhart asked.

Don shrugged. "Christ if I know."

Melanie studied the little gold figure inside, with its finger pointing at its mouth. "Harpocrates."

Eckhart blinked dumbly.

"The Graeco-Egyptian god of silence."

"I knew she'd know," Don said proudly. He wasn't so proud of her in all the other cases. "I've got an eye for this." It was just such a pity he didn't have an eye for the perpetrator.

"So what does it mean?" Eckhart asked. "Does it even mean anything?"

"To the person behind this," Melanie said, "it means everything."

Yet, it also meant something to her. A bound hand. A blinded eye. A covered ear. A silenced mouth. Her last words to Stephen came back to her like a ghost. "I can't talk right now." Maybe they were just idle words, a frantic declaration in the heat of the moment. Or maybe, just like the Tarot cards, they meant something more. Maybe, slowly by slowly, without any visible signs, the orchestrator of all of this was paralysing her too, in his own way, making her unable to see or speak, unable to do her job, unable to find him.

THE DEVIL
IN THE DETAILS

Despite how tired Melanie was, she spent the next few hours in the forensics lab with Carla O'Brien, their specialist in occult forensics. She'd already went over the items for prints, DNA, and other identifying features, but everything came up clean. Melanie wanted a second look.

"I presume you noticed the pattern," Carla said.

"Yeah."

"They've all got something to do with cutting off the senses."

"What sense have we got left?"

"Hmm?"

"Touch is gone. Sight is gone. Sound is gone. Taste is gone."

"So that leaves smell," Carla said, smiling. She always did smile no matter how horrible the case was. She got as much of a kick out of solving things as Melanie did, perhaps even more. "I guess we know what our next charm will be then."

"And then?" Melanie asked.

"And then what?"

"There's space for six charms on the bracelets."

"Yeah, I noticed that."

"So what sense does the last one cover?"

Carla bit her lip as she ruminated on the matter. Melanie did the same.

"The sixth sense," Melanie said in time.

"Many say that doesn't exist," Carla replied.

"It depends who you ask. I bet a survey of the Vowels would find most have experienced it in one form or another."

"So six symbols," Carla said, "covering the six senses."

"Maybe not just symbols."

"Why d'you say that?"

"I think there's magic involved." She paused. "You could say I have a sixth sense about it."

"Good thing we're not at the last charm then," Carla said. "So, you think the culprit is blocking out our senses with these? Hiding their trail?"

"Yeah. That's why we need to be quick, or it won't matter what clues we stumble upon. We won't even notice them."

Melanie put on her white cotton gloves before inspecting the items. Often she would be holding up bullets. It wasn't every day you got people dying from charms.

"They all have different origins," Carla said as she came over. She pointed with her little finger to each in turn. "This first one has Middle-Eastern origins. The second one is potentially Eastern European."

"It has a Sinti flair to it," Melanie noted.

"Then we move Far East with the monkey, then to Alexandria with the figurine."

"I wonder if this mix of cultures means something."

"It's hard to tell. It might be that the culprit just couldn't find a full set of applicable symbols from one pot, as it were."

"Or it's supposed to hint at mixed cultures," Melanie said. "Even Alexandria suggests that. It was the melting pot of the ancient world, where cultures met. My own background is kind of like that, a mix of cultures."

"I wondered about that," Carla said, "with the name. Isn't it Jewish?"

"My family adopted a new name after the War. We were said to have a variation of an Indian surname before that, but my grandparents wouldn't disclose it, for fear they'd be ostracised in the post-War events. There was a general feeling that Romani who fled the Nazis wouldn't be allowed to return or seek reparations. My grandmother kept referring to her family as 'the forgotten.'" Melanie sighed. "I guess even I forgot them, forgot my roots."

"You were born here in Ireland though, right?"

"Yes, my grandparents moved here during the war, then back to Germany after, but my parents stayed in Ireland. So I really do have a mix of roots. It's always made me unsure where I belong." She paused, staring at the charms. "Anyway, sorry. I got off track."

"No worries. I'm always curious about people," Carla said.

"So am I. I'm most curious about this killer."

"They're not a killer yet. The victims are still alive."

"For how long, though?"

"The first two … I wouldn't say long. Probably days at most."

Melanie's heart fell. "Let's focus, then." She really meant to just tell herself. The longer this went on for, the harder it was to focus, the hazier things became. It wasn't just her lack of sleep now. Her senses were getting blurred. Those little calling cards were working like a charm.

A LITTLE UNIVERSE

Melanie spent the next two hours studying the charms, turning them around, putting them under a microscope, bringing out all of the machines and tools Carla had used before, including x-rays, orgone generators, and dowsing rods. No matter how scientific or occult, nothing seemed to pick up anything. There were no fingerprints or identifying marks, no manufacturer's stamp or hint of origin, bar their distinct design. She told herself to consult some historians or specialists in this area, but wasn't sure that would turn up anything either. She kept looking, even when Carla closed up shop and left for the night.

"Sometimes it's better to go home and come back with fresh eyes," Carla said.

That was a problem for Melanie. Once she got it into her head, she couldn't get it out. Don sometimes called her "the bulldozer." She just kept on going, knocking away everything in her path. She feared that maybe the real clues could be found in the debris.

"Yeah," Melanie responded. "I could do with fresh eyes."

Yet still she stared at the charms.

"I guess that's a no then," Carla said with a laugh. "Well, just make sure you turn the lights off before you go. If they're left on all night, they could damage some of the specimens here." Carla had a bit of a museum curator in her. She said every human being was a collector at heart, but if that was so, then she was more human than most. To her, solving crimes came second to collecting evidence. Melanie just wanted the solutions. The means didn't matter. She'd bulldoze her way to the end.

Melanie gave a distracted wave goodbye, returning her full attention to the charms. She studied them further, until she started to doze off. She didn't even realise it when she found herself resting her head on her folded arms on the table, right next to the charms, dreaming evil dreams.

She dreamt of Stephen, dreamt of them fighting, yelling back and forth. She felt his strong hand on her arm, digging into the muscle, and her shaking it off. Then the feeling faded, until she felt nothing at all. One sense down. Then he seemed to fade into shadow, until she couldn't see him. Two. Then she couldn't hear his wrathful rebukes. Three. Then she couldn't speak her own. Four. Then, strong as anything, she could smell the horrid stench of his cigars. It was so strong, she could almost smell it off herself, like she often did when she left his apartment before they split up. She asked him many times to quit, but he always refused. As much as she bulldozed through, he was immovable. It was always doomed to fail.

The smell of cigars became so overpowering, it

seemed like nothing else existed except the fumes. Men and women were made of it. The world was made of it, with rolling hills of smoke. The sky was made of it, the water too. Even God was made of it. Somewhere, in that little universe, aroma was everything.

She woke, finding herself staring at the charms right in front of her nose. She blinked the sleep away, but noticed that the smell didn't fade. She sniffed deeply, still getting the whiff of cigars. She perked up, eyes wide, mind racing.

With only four charms there, not all of her senses were paralysed. Smell was perhaps the most overlooked of the five. Sometimes, no matter what you tried, you couldn't escape it. Melanie couldn't get it out of her nostrils. She couldn't get it out of her mind either. Now she knew who the perpetrator was.

PAYING A VISIT

When Melanie finally left the occult forensics lab, she found Eckhart waiting for her downstairs.

"You're late," he said.

"For what?"

"You said you wanted to check out some of the trinket stores to see if there are any matching charms on sale."

"Oh. Yes. Sorry, I forgot."

"You forgot?"

"I've had a lot on my mind."

"Yeah," Eckhart said. "I thought these charms were too."

"They are, but … can we take a rain-check on that? I think I need a nap first. I've been up all night."

"Okay, sure. Give me a call when you're ready. I might see if I can scout out these trinket shops myself." He grinned. "Who knows, might find a charm of my own."

Melanie headed off, but she didn't go home. She needed sleep, but she knew she'd never drift off now. She'd had her nap already. She didn't need more disturbing dreams.

She headed for Stephen's place. Normally she didn't make surprise visits, not to friends, but this couldn't wait, and she needed to catch him off guard. She also needed an excuse to be there.

She banged on the door.

"Who is it?" Stephen shouted from inside.

She decided not to answer, and ducked out of view of the spy hole.

Stephen opened up.

"We need to talk," Melanie said, pushing past him. She could bulldoze her way into a room as well.

"Woah! Jesus, Melanie. What are you doing here?"

Melanie had barely gotten inside before she got the pungent smell of cigars. The apartment reeked of it. She was sure she'd reek of it too by the time she left.

"I need a friendly ear," Melanie said.

"Why didn't you call?" Stephen asked, locking the door.

"I was passing by."

"Here? You don't patrol here. I know."

"You don't know everything about me or my cases."

"I know enough," Stephen said. "And you tell me plenty."

She couldn't deny that. As much as they didn't work as a couple, he was always a sympathetic ear, a shoulder to cry on. She could rely on him to be discreet. Or so she thought. Maybe he was using that information against her. She wasn't sure of anything any more.

She slumped down onto the sofa, crossing her legs. Stephen sauntered in after her, sitting across the way. He immediately reached for the cigar box on the table.

"What's this about?" he asked, lighting one up.

"You still smoke."

"Yeah."

"It's bad for you."

"So's a lotta things, melon. And anyway, blame Ernest. He got me smoking cigars in the first place."

"And dabbling in magic," Melanie said coolly. "That's bad for you too."

"I've had enough scolding from him over that. I don't need yours as well."

"Do you still do it?" she asked.

"What?"

"Magic."

"Of course. It's like a drug. Once you start, you can't stop."

Like killing people, Melanie thought.

"You all right, melon? You seem more on edge than usual."

"I'm just tired."

"You can kip here if you want. Got the spare room."

"No, I just wanted to chat."

"What about?"

"Do you ever use charms?"

"Charms?" The flicker of fire from the cigar illuminated his dark eyes. "What are you driving at?"

"I'm not driving at anything."

"You are. You always are."

"Just answer the question, Stephen."

"Well, yeah. I use charms. I use everything. A bit of this, a bit of that. You already know that."

She did, but she had to hear it from him. She wanted to see his reaction to her question. The problem was, if her vision had been clouded, then she might not have been seeing things as they really were. There wasn't a lot to go on. Just the smell. And a hunch. You couldn't jail people on a hunch. Not even with the Vowels testifying.

"Do you ever sell them?" she asked.

"Charms? No. But I give some away, if it suits me."

"To who?"

"To whoever. If I want more money, I might give one to my bank manager. They're talismans, little houses of magic. Sometimes you make them for yourself, and other times you make them work a little magic on someone else."

"Like me?"

"I never used any on you. What we had was real, warts and all."

"How would I know?"

Stephen shrugged. "I suppose you wouldn't." He paused. "Ernest would, though."

"If you didn't use them on him too."

Stephen laughed. "Are you serious? Jesus, melon, you've become a right fruit lately. You were better when you were a desk clerk. Do you really think I could get through Ernest's defences? And, y'know, he isn't even the greatest of those in his circle."

That only added another thread to the web for Melanie. What if it was someone in Ernest's circle?

Her heart sank at the next question: what if it was Ernest himself? It didn't seem right, but then nothing about this did. Who would want to do any of this at all?

"Do you think I did it?" Stephen asked, puffing on his cigar. He was awfully relaxed for such a loaded question, but then he found those cigars relaxing.

Melanie looked at him, but said nothing.

"Do you think I did those charm crimes you talked about?"

Melanie couldn't remember just how much she'd told him about things. They'd met up before, early on, when it was just two victims. She'd looked to him for solace, for advice. She wasn't sure if it was really just her instincts that pointed in his direction.

"I don't know," Melanie said eventually.

"Jesus." He dabbed the cigar out in the ashtray. The smoke and stench lingered.

"I don't know what to think, Stephen. I'm lost." She wasn't entirely sure if she was just revealing herself to the perpetrator, if maybe this was what he wanted.

"Well, take me in then. I'm not gonna fight you."

Melanie took a deep breath, then sighed. She was so sure before. Now she wasn't. Things had become muddled again. She wondered if her past, and her friendship with him, was clouding things. The only thing that was clear was the smell, and that otherworldly sense that something wasn't adding up.

She stared at the cigar box, which was still open. Her mind wandered.

Stephen noticed her staring. "What, don't tell me

you want one."

She kept staring, ignoring his question. Then something twigged in her mind.

"Are you still on two a day?"

"Yeah, got my old routine. Why?"

"And you get a new box on the first of every month."

"God, Melanie. What's this about?"

"We've got five days left in this month. That should be ten cigars. There's only nine."

"So?"

"Did you smoke extra?"

"No. You know I'm a creature of habit. This is my first today, and I'll have another tonight. It's always been two, always will be."

"So, with the one you take tonight, that leaves eight cigars to cover five more days. You're two short."

"Yeah, I gave Don and Toby one each when they were over last week."

Melanie's jaw almost dropped to the floor. "Don and Toby," she said dumbly.

"Yeah, why?"

Melanie got up without answering, vanishing out the door in a flutter of fabric. The door creaked closed behind her and Stephen locked it again. He strolled back to the sofa, sitting in Melanie's spot. He took the cigar back up, relit it, then kicked back and smiled.

WHO TO TRUST?

Melanie went outside and sat in the car. She sat in silence for a moment, her mind spinning. Then she hammered her fists down on the dashboard in frustration. It seemed the closer she got to a solution, the farther away she felt. She thought she'd narrowed down the list. Now it was wider than ever. Now it included her comrades in the OIU.

She pursed her lips, shaking her head. *It can't be*, she told herself. It didn't make any sense. Why would Don or Eckhart do something like this? There had to be a reason. There had to be an answer.

She dialled Eckhart's number on her phone.

"Hey, you ready?"

"For what?" Melanie asked.

"The charm shops. I thought that's where we were going next."

"Oh. Yes. No, actually, Toby, I'm chasing another lead."

"Cool. What've you got?"

"Did you meet with Stephen last week?"

"Huh?"

"Stephen."

"I know who Stephen is. What do you mean?"

"He said you and Don paid him a visit last week."

"Ah, right. He told you that, huh?"

"Well?"

"I wasn't supposed to tell you this," Eckhart said, "but he came up as a *person of interest* in another case. It was a bit vague, but we wanted to check it out."

"Why didn't you tell me?"

"Well, with your history with him and all, Don thought it best to leave you out of the loop."

"And what did you think best?"

"I thought it best to follow the big guy's orders."

"What was the case?"

"Mel, I can't go into that. You know how these things go. You're too close to him."

"Fine," she said. "Did you smoke a cigar with him?"

"Yeah. He offered. Thought it best not to say no, given the circumstances. And you know Don. He wouldn't refuse a cigar for his life. Hell, I had to give him mine after two puffs. I couldn't stomach the stuff."

Melanie was silent.

"You still there, Mel?"

"Yeah."

"Want me to come over?"

"No. I think I need to go it alone for a bit. I'll call you later."

Alone was the perfect word. She wasn't sure she could rely on her partner now, or the guy in charge. She started to see their remarks in a different light, and wondered what they were keeping from her. She wasn't sure she should even go back to the station, and yet she also thought maybe she shouldn't let it seem like she knew too much.

CHARM DEALER

Melanie headed into the City Centre on the Luas tram, then made for the small market stalls and dingy shops of the city's occult quarter. People sold all sorts of stuff there, much of it aimed at tourists, a lot of it junk. It was the perfect place to find odds and ends, the perfect place to find charms.

There were several dealers of trinkets along Carter Street. Dusk was setting in, so some of them were starting to close up. She had to hurry past the bustle to avoid missing anything. She scoured the stalls with her eyes, digging through some baskets and boxes of jewels, gems, and little figurines. Much of it was plastic or pewter. Nothing had quite the same look or feel as those charms used in the attacks.

"Lookin' for somethin' in particular, love?" one of the street sellers asked.

"Where's the best place for charms here?"

"Charms? I've got a few of those here."

"I need the biggest selection, preferably old charms."

The seller furrowed her brow. "That'd be Bits

and Bobs on the corner then. Bob O'Malley runs the place. You tell him I sent you. Won't get you a discount, mind, but tell him all the same."

Melanie thanked the woman and headed over to the tiny corner shop. She would have walked right past if she wasn't looking for it.

There were ragged carpets hanging on the walls inside. Maybe the owner thought they were tapestries. The whole place was dark, with much of the windows obscured by an array of items, some on the sills, some hanging from the top. The place was very dusty, and musky too. There was a faint scent of incense.

"What can I do ya for?" Bob asked.

"The lady outside said you're the best place for charms."

"That I am. Got all sorts here. You want friendship bracelets? Something for a communion gift? I've got ready-made bits in gift boxes, hey presto, ready to go. Or I can do you something unique. We do hand-carved medallions with your name on it, great for birthdays. Or pick and mixes too for the more generic trinkets."

"This is going to sound odd," Melanie said.

"Try me."

Melanie cleared her throat. "Do you sell noses?"

The dealer raised an eyebrow. "Do I sell noses?"

"Charms in the shape of a nose, or symbolic of a nose, or … something like that."

"No, I don't think so," he said. "I can't see them being very popular."

Melanie must have looked very dejected, because the shopkeeper got overly sympathetic, coming around the front and taking her hand.

"Now, don't you worry, young miss," he said with a twitch of his moustache. "There could be a nose in here somewhere if you're dead set on it. I get buckets of bits and bobs coming in every week. Nary the time to check 'em all. Why, come on down here and we'll have a look for ya."

He led her further into the store, which was bigger than it looked, through some of the aisles that got even less light from the obscured windows. He pointed out boxes here and there, which he said were worth rooting through, and then led her around to another aisle, where she stumbled upon Eckhart, who was already searching through some of the boxes there.

"Toby," she said, surprised.

"Mel? I thought you weren't coming?"

"I … I got a moment free."

The shopkeeper looked back and forth between them. "I'll leave you to it then." He ambled off, and the jovial air he created faded, leaving behind the cooler air between Melanie and Eckhart.

"Have you found anything?" Eckhart asked her.

"Not yet."

"I got this," he said, holding up what looked like an identical charm to the bound hand found on the first victim. Melanie took it from him. "There's a whole box of them over there," he added.

"So it's not rare."

"Doesn't appear to be," Eckhart said. "But that doesn't really help us though, because it means anyone could have bought it. Hell, there's probably hundreds out there."

"See if you can find the other ones."

Then she paused, as she thought she heard a familiar voice. Eckhart was about to say something, but she shushed him. She gestured for him to duck low.

"What's up?" he whispered.

"Listen," she whispered back.

Eckhart squinted as he strained his hearing. "Is that … Carla?"

Melanie peeked between some of the boxes, spotting Carla at the till. The shopkeeper had a box of trinkets and charms already packed for her. They cracked a few jokes. It seemed Carla was a regular. As she left, Melanie and Eckhart looked at each other.

"You don't think—?" Eckhart began.

Melanie shrugged. The list of suspects was growing longer. Carla was so sweet and innocent, no one would think twice about her. She could get away with murder.

The shopkeeper hobbled around to them, doing a double take as he spotted them both crouching to the floor.

"D-d-did you find anything?" he asked.

They had, though it wasn't what they came in for.

APPROACHING
THE EDGE

They left the shop empty-handed, looking both ways to see if they could spot where Carla went. Melanie didn't know where she lived, but was confident Eckhart could get the details from Don. Maybe over another cigar.

Carla had vanished just as quickly as she came, along with her box of trinkets. She might have been right that everyone was a collector at heart, but not everyone was a killer. She didn't seem the type, but then they never did.

Eckhart's phone rang. He answered it, then handed it to Melanie.

"It's Don," he said. "He said he tried calling you."

She forgot she'd turned her phone off. She didn't want to talk to anyone. Yet here she was with all the old crew. She just couldn't escape them.

"What's up?" she asked Don.

"You better sit for this."

"What's wrong?"

"We've got victim number five now."

She sighed and shook her head. "Another one," she told Eckhart.

She almost missed what Don said next. "Melanie, listen. It's Stephen."

ALMOST A FULL
COLLECTION

They raced back to the station, charged down the corridors, then burst into the room where they were keeping Stephen's paralysed body. He was just as bad as the suspended man, and there was already talk of sending him downstairs.

"Have you got anything?" Melanie asked Don.

Don almost hid behind his clipboard. He wasn't good with the mushy stuff. Maybe he thought she was going to break down on seeing Stephen. She wasn't, though she was silently breaking. The whole case was causing some cracks.

"Nothing," Don said. "Just the usual."

"A nose?"

"Yes. Looks like something Neolithic, a fossil of some kind. The nostrils are now filled with the same stone as the rest of it."

"So that's smell gone."

Don raised an eyebrow.

"Nothing. We've pretty much run out of time."

"There's still one to go," Eckhart said. He was circling the bed that Stephen was laying still on, with his eyes forever open. The look of fear in his face was frozen there. It was enough to make you shiver.

"I hate to say it," Don said, "but at least that'll be the end of it."

"What makes you so sure?" Eckhart asked.

"I presume it'll all end once all six charms are in place."

"Or the perpetrator can go on doing this without fear of ever being caught," Melanie said. "All our senses will be blocked then. We could have a mountain of evidence, but we wouldn't even know it's there."

"Speaking of which," Don said. "I better bring this up to the lab." He held up a small plastic bag with the fifth charm in it.

"I'll take it," Melanie said. "To add to Carla's collection."

BACK IN THE LAB

Melanie headed up to the lab, where she found Carla whistling away as she carefully classified samples and evidence into a huge cabinet full of little plastic drawers. When she caught sight of Melanie clutching the plastic bag, she jumped up and down, clapping her hands together like a child on her birthday.

"Oooh, another one," she said. She took the bag and held it up. "And we were right. That's the five conventional senses down."

"Where did you put the other ones?"

"They're in a box on the table over there. I thought you already looked at them."

"I want one last look."

Melanie put on her white gloves, then took the four items out carefully. She sniffed them, one by one. There was no smell. That overwhelming stench of cigars was gone, just like Stephen was—though he wasn't quite dead yet.

"There was a smell off these before," Melanie said.

"Really? I didn't get anything."

"It was pretty strong."

"Well, I tend to work with strong chemicals. My sense of smell isn't that great now."

Melanie wasn't sure if she believed her. For all she knew, Carla could have scrubbed the charms clean.

"Ever collect charms yourself, Carla?"

"Oh, I collect everything. You should see my house."

I'd like to, Melanie thought. She wondered about getting that address.

"Y'know," Carla said, smiling as she held the stone nose up to her own, "if I didn't have a job like this, I don't know what I'd do."

Melanie wondered about that. *Maybe you'd kill someone.*

OLD SCHOOL

Melanie was as uncertain as ever about the case, and she needed certainty fast, before the final window closed and everything became a permanent blur. She decided to stop by the National Library after closing hours, when she could talk to Mr. Constant.

"You're becoming a nuisance, you know," the magician said as he stepped outside.

"Can I come in?"

"We're supposed to be closed."

"Supposed to be, yes."

Mr. Constant grumbled and led her in, down a winding corridor, and into a small, cosy room with a fireplace. He cast some logs in and struck a match.

"Can't you just … click your fingers?" Melanie asked.

Mr. Constant scoffed. "I *can*, but that would be a waste, and a violation of my oaths. I didn't learn magic to make my life more comfortable."

"But it helps."

Mr. Constant stared over his glasses. "What in the blazes are you doing back here, Melanie? I hope you didn't put my name in any reports. I get enough attention from that rabble of yours as is."

"I'm lost, Ernest."

"Well, I can see *that*."

"This case—"

"Now, don't you start dragging me further into that. You already got me involved quite enough! I don't want to know any more. The more I know, the more I'm compelled to act, and I can't act without skirting the edges of my oaths. I'm not supposed to be getting involved in all this mundane malarkey."

"But it's not *mundane*," Melanie protested. "There's some magic going on, blinding me. I feel like I'm close, but all my senses are getting shut off. Can't you do something? Can't you do some divination or remote viewing, or whatever it is you do?"

"I'd like to, Melanie, but there are rules that you know nothing about, and they can't be broken without dire penalties. Malik is an example of that."

"But you helped with him."

"We had unfinished business. If it wasn't him, I wouldn't have been able to help you."

"What about advice?"

"I can give that," Mr. Constant said. "The question is: can you heed it?"

"This magic with the charms—"

"Don't tell me the details. Keep it vague."

Melanie sighed. "Oh, it's pretty vague all right."

"Go on."

"It's blocking my senses."

"So unblock them."

"How?"

"Everything has its opposite, Melanie."

"What do you mean?"

"Whatever was done to block your senses, simply do the reverse of it."

"I'm not sure how."

"Not all your senses are blocked. I can tell you that right now."

"I've got my intuition, but I'm unsure."

"Put aside all the doubts and suspicions, all the biases and opinions. Get to the kernel of pure experiential knowledge. Then you'll know what to do."

"You weren't wrong about you liking things vague," Melanie said.

Mr. Constant chortled. "That's as clear as it gets in this world, Melanie. If you want it any clearer, you have to make it yourself."

FIVE OF HER OWN

Melanie went back to Bits and Bobs the next day. She was becoming just as much a regular as Carla was. She just hoped that didn't come with another, darker hobby.

"Back again," the owner said, with his now familiar smile. As dark as that store was, there was a brightness in him. He clearly loved what he did. His enthusiasm was infectious.

"Yeah," Melanie said.

"I found something a bit like what you were looking for before."

"Oh?"

He pulled a small ornament from behind the counter. It looked like a miniature Pinocchio with a long nose, and a hook at the top to hang it up.

"Not sure it quite fits the bill, but … it's got a very prominent nose."

"Thanks. I'm actually looking for something else this time. Or rather a few things."

"Well, now! Let's see what we can find for ya."

"I need an open eye and an open mouth for

starters." She took a fifty Euro note out of her pocket and placed it on the counter. "Can you help me look?"

"Put that away!" the shopkeeper cried. "I'll help for the helpin'! An eye and a mouth, you say?"

"Open. They have to be open."

"Sure thing, sweetie. You try down the far end and I'll start here."

They scoured the shop, and Bob only paused his search to momentarily help another customer who came in. By the time night fell, they had dozens of potential items that fit the bill, some in stone or metal, others in porcelain or plastic.

"Catch of the day," Bob said with a chuckle. "Anything of use?"

Melanie rummaged through the pile, plucking out a copper Eye of Horus, an African carving of a man with a giant open mouth, with the tongue sticking out, a Hamsa symbol with no bindings, and a little iron figure of a man holding his hand to his ear. That covered four of the senses.

"These will work wonders," she said. "And here, throw in that Pinocchio too. The bigger the nose, the more you can smell, right?"

Bob laughed. "Why not?"

He packed the trinkets up carefully in coloured tissue. Melanie paid him, and insisted on a tip, and for the first time since all of this started, she felt much more at ease. She wasn't sure if it was the fact that she now had a plan or if Bob's good nature was just rubbing off on her. With him around, it seemed like anything was possible. In the Hibernian Hollows, anything was.

REVERSAL

The cheer faded a little by the time Melanie got home. She brought the charms to her coffee table, where her grandmother's Tarot cards were still arranged. She'd barely been home lately. She couldn't complain though. Lack of sleep was nothing compared to what the paralysis victims were going through.

She laid out the items from left to right, then stared at them for a moment. It was odd to think that such lifeless, little things could have such effect. Of course, the charm was just a vessel. It was the magic you filled it with that did the trick.

Melanie was no magician, and she only had an inkling of how to reverse the process taken by the culprit of these crimes. She hoped that inkling would be enough.

She started with the last one, symbolic of smell. She thought it best that everything be done in reverse. She almost wondered if she should say the words backwards too, but thought better of it. The words she used she didn't understand, more of that ancient,

111

indecipherable tongue her grandmother had taught her. She never thought she would be using them so much, never thought she would be looking so often to her roots.

For a while, nothing seemed to be happening. A sense of doubt began to well up deep inside her, gnawing away at her prior confidence. Her grandmother had warned her not to give in to doubt, and Mr. Constant had echoed those words. So far, Melanie had been doubting almost everything, even her own sanity.

The words rolled off her tongue like thunder. The room darkened and brightened. There was electricity in the air. The little trinkets buzzed with energy. The little Pinnochio almost seemed like a real boy. The iron man almost seemed to wiggle his ear. The African figure almost seemed to grin and loll his tongue. The Eye of Horus almost seemed to wink at her. The Hamsa hand almost seemed to wave. One by one they came to life with purpose. One by one, she undid the spell on her and everyone around her.

She smiled as the astral walls came down, as she finally found some success, but the smile quickly faded as her intuition guided her to memories that she didn't even know she had, to words said, to sights seen. Things that seemed normal now seemed odd. She had a sinking feeling in her chest.

She called Don.

"It's the middle of the night, for Christ's sake," he growled.

"Sorry, but it's important."

"The case can wait, Melanie."

"It really can't, Don."

"Okay, then shoot."

"That time you went to Stephen's place with Toby—"

"I thought it was about the case?"

"It is. Hear me out. That time you went there … what was it for?"

"Eckhart had a suspicion Stephen was up to something. Christ, maybe he was. Maybe he was behind this the whole time, and couldn't take it in the end and did it to himself."

"So you didn't give the order to investigate Stephen?"

"No. It was Eckhart's idea. He asked me to keep it on the down low in case you let something slip to Stephen that he was being watched. I had Eckhart stake out his place for days, but he didn't see anyone come or go."

"That's all I needed to know."

"Are you serious? You woke me up for that?"

"No, Don. I just needed some confirmation. I know who did all this."

"I'm listening."

"It was Toby."

FORGOTTEN

In the OIU headquarters, everything was shut down for the night. Yet someone walked through those halls, largely unnoticed. The shoes clattered off the ground in an ominous way, one by one, like the march of Death.

The figure entered the room where Stephen was kept, still wide awake with terror. He was one of the few not sleeping. He stared helplessly as the figure circled the bed.

"So," Eckhart said, pulling a slip of paper up that was taped to the bottom of Stephen's bed. "You're destined for downstairs, it seems. I could have told you you were destined for that all along. You were never going to get back together with her, you know. It was never going to happen."

Eckhart took out an apple, and a knife. He let the faint light in the room glint off the sharp edge. Then he took a slice, using the knife to scoop it into his mouth. He did this again, slice by slice, showing the knife each time. To Stephen, completely helpless on the table, it must have been torture. As far as he knew,

Eckhart could do anything to him.

Eckhart finished his apple, then dragged a chair across the floor, letting it screech. He didn't have to be quiet. No one would hear him. He plopped down beside Stephen, bringing their faces close to each other.

"You know, you ruined her," he said. "You took the chance I should have had, and you blew it. She didn't want me. She didn't even know I existed. But you … you kept on calling, and she kept on coming. You just wouldn't go away."

Eckhart stood up sharply. "Well, it's only a matter of time now, and the clock is ticking fast. Soon enough, you'll be forgotten, just like she forgot me."

COMPLETING
THE CIRCLE

M elanie called Eckhart several times, but he didn't answer. Normally he answered in an instant, as if he had been waiting for her call.

She raced towards the station, where Don was also heading, hoping she would find her partner there, hoping she would be able to catch him and end this once and for all. Yet there was still another charm to add to the bracelet, still another body to add to a body bag.

It was approaching midnight, so Bits and Bobs was closed, but Bob was still there, sorting through his new inventory. He hummed away to himself as he cast various trinkets into different coloured boxes.

The shop was darker now that night came, and Bob was working by candlelight. For whatever reason, he felt at home in the dark, tucked away from sight, just like so many of those little charms were.

He was so absorbed by his work that he didn't

hear someone creeping up behind him. By the time the floor creaked, he tried to turn, then froze, and everything went black for a second. When he could see again, he saw a man standing there, his left hand held palm outward, glowing blue, and his right hand dangling a little chain with a spirit wheel charm hanging on the end.

"Sorry, Bob," Eckhart said. "It's nothing personal."

MINUTES TO MIDNIGHT

M elanie arrived at the station not long after Don. She charged in, finding him turning on the computers in the Operations Room.

"Are you sure about this?" he asked her when she entered.

"Yes," she said. "I can't believe I didn't see it before."

"I'm putting a lot of faith in you. You better be right."

As happy as Melanie was to finally have the culprit in their sights, she really hoped she was wrong.

"He's due back in tomorrow morning," Don said. "We can spring a trap."

"Tomorrow might be too late, Don. We need to find him tonight."

"I'll track his phone."

"His phone's off."

"That doesn't matter. All mobiles from the Vowels have been rigged to transmit a signal all the time."

"Nice to know," Melanie said sardonically.

"Well, it proved useful this time."

A blinking dot appeared on the map on the screen. Don zoomed in as far as he could.

"Carter Street," he said. "What's he doing there at this time of night?"

"Finishing what he started."

Melanie raced back outside. She needed to finish things first.

MIDNIGHT

It was lucky it was late, because there was no one on the road. She broke every light, ignored every sign. All that mattered was the destination. She only hoped she wasn't too late.

When she arrived at Carter Street, she barely stopped the car before hopping out, leaving the door open. She charged up to the front door, trying the handle. It was locked. She thumped the door with her fist, then kicked it.

"Toby! Are you in there? Bob! Let me in!"

Inside the store, just moments before Melanie arrived, Eckhart was finishing up his work with Bob. Eckhart hoisted himself up onto the counter, dangling his legs like a child.

"You might be wondering why," he said. He shrugged. "Why not? Sometimes you just reach breaking point. Either you snap or you snap others. Kill or be killed. I never felt like I mattered. Well, I matter now, don't I? To you, definitely, and to the others. And maybe, in time, I'll matter to her."

He paused, as if waiting for Bob's response. Bob couldn't respond. The magic was working faster than ever. It was exhausting, but also exhilarating.

"What's that?" Eckhart asked, hearing the implied response. "Who's she, you ask? The girl of my dreams, or so I thought. She only ever seemed to look at me when I was dreaming. All the other times, I was just the guy driving the car, the guy filing the reports, the guy watching on as she picked the wrong man. I tried to warn her."

He pulled a photo out of his inside coat pocket. It showed Melanie, smiling. She didn't smile as often as he'd like, and maybe she wasn't going to smile about this, but she'd pay attention. He scoffed at the memory that she didn't even know he was taking the photo, that she was so wrapped up in her own little world, she never noticed him.

"She's beautiful, huh?" he said, holding the photo up to Bob. Bob could do nothing but look. "She doesn't think she is, you know. She thinks she's a mutt, but I think the gods got it right when they mixed the ingredients that made her. I told her that, but she didn't listen. She never listened."

He hopped down, putting the photo away. He drew up close to poor, old Bob and flicked him on the forehead.

"Do you feel that?" he asked. "No? Well, that's what it feels like to be me. I'm like this little bee buzzing around, but no one hears me, and no one feels me. So I've gotta sting someone. Again, it isn't personal."

He heard a sudden thumping at the door,

followed by Melanie's voice.

"And would ya look at that?" Eckhart said. "Right on cue."

He wandered over to the door, listened to the frantic thumping for a moment more, then opened up. Melanie saw him good and proper then. It was like, for the first time, she really looked.

Eckhart smiled a sickly smile. "*Now* you notice me."

TOO MANY QUESTIONS

M elanie immediately pulled her gun on Eckhart. It took a lot of effort not to also pull the trigger. It wasn't just the heinous crimes. It was the lies. It was the betrayal.

"Back away!" she warned him.

He backed away, charm in hand.

"Try anything with that and I'll blast your hand off."

"What if it was a charm to protect me from bullets?" Eckhart quipped. Even now, in a situation like this, he was still cracking jokes. No one was laughing.

"Is it?" Melanie asked. She couldn't be sure of anything any more.

"No. Even I can't make a charm for that."

"Why?" Melanie asked. She had too many questions, but they mostly boiled down to that one word.

"You really don't know, huh? That's a perfect example of it all."

"Of all what?"

Eckhart's eyes bulged. "Of how you never pay any attention to me. I might as well be a sack of grain sitting next to you. You probably wouldn't even know the difference."

"That's not true."

"It is to me. Any time I tried to open up to you, you brushed me aside. Don said you were a bulldozer. Well, I say you're a tidal wave. You washed away everything in your path, including me."

"That's not fair, Toby."

"Don't talk to me about what's not fair!"

"I didn't ask to be your partner, Toby."

"I didn't ask to be yours either, but at least I wanted it. At least I cared."

"I cared, Toby. I *care*. That's why this hurts so much."

"So you feel me now, do you? Look what I had to do to get your attention, to get your focus." He gestured to poor, old Bob, his latest victim, and she hoped his last. She wondered if maybe instead that would be her.

"Why didn't you just talk to me, Toby?" she pleaded. "Why did you have to do *this*?"

He shook his head. "I did talk. You never listened. I used all the senses, but you were closed to me. You shunned me. I tried to reach out, but you never reached back. You don't know what it's like, Mel. You don't know what it's like to go through life and feel totally ignored."

"You're not the only one with problems, Toby."

He scoffed. "Damn right I'm not. There's six more who've caught your paralysis. Just like you, they can't see or hear or feel. All I did was show how bad it is, made it … more tangible."

"Well, I got the message—"

"Did you, though? It was a simple message. Why is that I had to hammer it home?"

"I'm paying attention now, Toby."

"For all the wrong reasons." He sighed. "And maybe, you know … maybe it's too late."

"It's not too late, Toby. No one's dead yet. You can undo this."

He looked despondently to the floor. "It won't change anything though, will it? You'll never love me, not like I love you."

"I'll love you less if you let these people die. They're innocent, Toby. I'm the guilty party here. Punish me, not them."

"I don't want to *punish* you, Mel! That's not what this is about."

"I get what it's about, but I need you to let them free."

"I'm not even sure I can," he said.

"How did you make them like this? The charms?"

"The charms were for you, Mel. I knew you'd pay attention to those. I knew even Don wouldn't refuse to hand this case to you."

"Then how did you do it, Toby?"

Eckhart made a gesture like a stage magician. "Magic."

"I never knew you were into that."

"Well, like I said, you never listen. And everyone's got a little magic in them, Mel. You should know."

STAND-OFF

"**P**ut the gun away," Eckhart urged.

"No."

"This isn't going to end like that, Mel. Not with lead."

"I hope it ends with you reversing what you did."

"And what, just pretend like nothing's happened?"

"I can't do that," she said.

"You could do it before. One awkward word, then let's all just go back to normal. No happy families, just two co-workers, typing up reports no one'll read, living meaningless lives, soon to be forgotten. Well, I won't be forgotten, Mel. *People will remember me.*"

"Not for the right reasons, Toby."

He smiled. "Are there any? We don't remember the heroes in this world, Mel. We only remember the villains."

"That's not true."

"Open your eyes, Mel! This is the world we live in."

"Tell me how you did it, Toby. Tell me how to save them."

"Go back in time," Eckhart said with a laugh. "But first, put the gun away."

They stared at each other for a moment, and Melanie refused. Then, with a suddenness that surprised her, Eckhart made a gesture and spoke aloud a single, indecipherable word. The gun slipped from her hand and floated over to his, growing swiftly smaller as it did. By the time he grasped it, it was nothing more than a little gun-shaped charm.

"You know, my family used to make these," he said. "Not guns. Charms. Then they too were forgotten. The modern world steamrolled over the past, just like you did. No one had time for that. We only wore trinkets for show. The meaning was gone … forgotten."

"I didn't know—"

"You didn't listen! I told you some of this before. Then it went back to you, always back to you. And you know what, Mel? I didn't even mind. I *wanted* it to go back to you. To me, you were all that mattered. What's worse is that despite all this, I kind of feel like you still are."

Melanie didn't know what to say to that.

"I know there's probably no hope for us," Eckhart said. He paused and looked at her, mouth open just a little, as if he was hoping she would correct him. "No Romeo and Juliet here, huh? There might be two dead partners, but … never lovers."

He had barely uttered those words when there was the sound of a gunshot. Melanie jumped, thinking Eckhart had somehow fired that little trinket. When she regained her wits, she saw Don enter the building, gun raised. Eckhart stumbled backwards, clutching his chest, then fell to the floor in a pool of blood.

SOLUTION

Melanie ran to Eckhart. Part of her had some sliver of concern for him still, even now, but much of her just needed him to tell her how to undo what he had done.

"No, no, no," she cried. She held her hand down on the wound, feeling the blood leak out around her fingers.

"I guess I was wrong," Eckhart said. "It does end with lead." He held up the tiny gun to her. "Here. Finish me off, will ya?"

"Please, Toby. Tell me how to set them free."

"I can't."

"Please. Some of them are just kids. Don't let it end like this."

"I mean … I'm not sure how."

Melanie shook her head, dumbfounded.

"I didn't learn how," Eckhart said.

Melanie held his head up. "You have to know."

He smiled. "This is the first time I've been in your arms, you know."

"Focus, Toby. There are six people whose lives are

129

in danger."

"It doesn't matter, Mel. This world … we're all just passers-through."

"It matters to them, Toby. It … it matters to me."

Eckhart coughed. He sounded weaker already. Even his hand on her arm was growing limp.

"Stay with me, Toby. Tell me how to undo it."

"I said I can't."

"Then tell me how you did it."

"You can't fix everything, Mel."

"I just need to fix this. Please, Toby."

So he told her, though it was a struggle for him. He told her of the symbols used, and the words, and how to correctly intone them. He taught her the gestures, which seemed similar to some taught by Melanie's grandmother. He gave her the secrets of magic that others might withhold, or might require that she take a pledge of secrecy for. He told her everything, because finally, to him, she was listening.

"Remember me, Mel," he said, and those were his final words.

Eckhart's hand slipped down, and Don placed his own on Melanie's shoulder.

"He's gone."

Melanie gulped back her tears. She knew she would never forget him, though now the memories were scarred. She also knew the case wasn't closed yet. She still had work to do.

UNDOING THE DAMAGE

Not all the damage could be undone. Some scars couldn't be unmade. She felt her heart was a little colder, her faith in people a little sapped. Eckhart had done a bit of paralysing there. But this wasn't about her, even if he had said it was. For her, it was about those six innocent people, dragged into someone else's problems.

She got permission from Don to take the six charms from the evidence locker and bring them home. She laid them out with her own ones and spent some time working through the words Eckhart had given her, and finding the opposites for them. She had to rely a lot on intuition, and the help of a journal her grandmother kept, which she dug out of the attic. She consulted the Tarot several times throughout the process, recognising her Knight of Swords, seeing Death come up here and there. It was definitely the end of something all right. She just hoped it wasn't a literal end for those poor people too.

By the end of the day she had developed a ritual that seemed like the opposite process that Eckhart used, assuming he hadn't been lying to her. She desperately wanted to call Mr. Constant for advice, but she knew he wouldn't comment on magical techniques. He had already told her plenty in his roundabout way.

During the ritual, she felt that sense of otherworldliness again, a connection to something higher, even the sense of finding the kernel of herself amidst the chaos. The charms came to life, or she found the hidden life within them, and she decharged the ones used by Eckhart, while seeing the victims in her mind's eye, gradually regaining feeling.

She had Don on call, because she wasn't sure she had what it would take. Don never sounded so happy in his life. All six victims had fully recovered. Physically, at least. The magic was undone, but the memories were still there.

There was no chance Eckhart would be forgotten.

41

A PLACE IN THE WORLD

If life was strange during that week, it was surreal the week after. She typed up a report that she would have normally given Eckhart to do. She typed his name in far too many places, in all those places where there was only a blank in her mind before.

Don was different too. What lack of confidence he had in her was gone. She'd proved herself in a way that it seemed he never thought she would, and yet he gave the impression that he always believed in her, that he knew she'd eventually pull through. Some cases required subtlety, and some required a bulldozer. She'd be there for those.

She paid a visit to Mr. Constant, eager to glean some extra little nuggets of insight from him. She felt she'd need them. Out of all her senses, that sixth one was tingling like crazy. In the Vowels, there'd be no end of cases where she'd need an esoteric edge.

Mr. Constant held a book on his lap while Melanie talked. For some of it, it almost seemed like he'd already heard it all, like he knew all along. He was the master of silence and secrecy, a master magician.

He kept his cards close to his chest.

"It's funny," Melanie told him. "This past week, I've felt lost. My whole life, actually. I know it sounds odd, and maybe even a little selfish, but it kind of feels like my entire history was pared down into the events of last week."

"That doesn't sound odd to me," Mr. Constant said with a glimmer in his eye.

"I never felt I fit in. Not even in the OIU. Well, maybe I'm not supposed to."

"What makes you say that?"

"I've wondered about my place in this world for so long. There are so many threads that make up my background, linking me to different places, different peoples. I used to think that was a problem, that it diluted everything, so that I never truly belonged. But now I see it makes up the tapestry of who I am. Maybe I'm not supposed to be just a round plug in a round hole, or any other shape. There are enough people like that. Maybe my place is somewhere in the middle, wandering the crossroads, walking a bit of all paths."

"So you've learned a bit then," Mr. Constant said, nodding proudly.

She smiled. "Maybe that's where I can help the most."

THE END

About the Author

Dean F. Wilson was born in Dublin, Ireland in 1987. He started writing at age 11, and has since become a *USA Today* and *Wall Street Journal* Bestselling Author.

He is the author of the *Children of Telm* epic fantasy trilogy, the *Great Iron War* steampunk series, the *Coilhunter Chronicles* science-fiction western series, the *Hibernian Hollows* urban fantasy series, and the *Infinite Stars* space opera series.

Dean previously worked as a journalist, primarily in the field of technology. He has written for *TechEye*, *Thinq*, *V3*, *VR-Zone*, *ITProPortal*, *TechRadar Pro*, and *The Inquirer*.

www.deanfwilson.com